More inspiring reads
by Rosanne Parry

Heart of a Shepherd
Second Fiddle
Written in Stone

the TuRn Of the TiDe

WITHDRAWN

ROSANNE PARRY

Random House New York

Text copyright © 2016 by Rosanne Parry
Jacket art copyright © 2016 by Julie McLaughlin
Map copyright © 2016 by Jennifer Thermes

Visit us on the Web! randomhousekids.com

Educators and librarians, for a variety of teaching tools, visit us at RHTeachersLibrarians.com

Library of Congress Cataloging-in-Publication Data
Parry, Rosanne.
The turn of the tide / Rosanne Parry.—First edition.
pages cm
Summary: After a devastating tsunami in Japan, cousins Jet and Kai spend the summer together in Astoria, Oregon, training for the Young's Bay Treasure Island sailboat race and become close friends in the process.
ISBN 978-0-375-86972-3 (hardcover : alk. paper) — ISBN 978-0-375-96972-0 (lib. bdg. : alk. paper) — ISBN 978-0-375-98535-5 (ebook)
[1. Cousins—Fiction. 2. Friendship—Fiction. 3. Sailing—Fiction. 4. Racially mixed people—Fiction. 5. Japanese Americans—Fiction. 6. Oregon—Fiction.] I. Title.
PZ7.P248Tu 2016
[Fic]—dc23 2014047701

Printed in the United States of America
10 9 8 7 6 5 4 3 2 1
First Edition

For my cousins,
my life's companions,
with gratitude and joy

Exultation is the going

Of an inland soul to sea—

Past the Houses—

Past the Headlands—

Into deep Eternity

—Emily Dickinson

WITHDRAWN

1

WHEN THE EARTH broke open, there was a noise that came before the quake. It was so deep Kai felt it on his skin almost before he heard it. It came before the crack of falling trees, before the hard rain of broken glass, even before the pop and whoosh of blue fire when the transformer behind the playground blew. One boom like a single beat from the *ōdaiko,* the big drum at the temple, only sounded for the most important festivals of the year. That beat passed through Kai's body like a wave of radiation, quick as lightning, invisible, irreversible.

Kai knew at once what he must do and what it would cost him even if he succeeded. It was a maverick choice, one that would mark him as even more of an outsider, a *hāfu,* neither properly Japanese nor glamorously American. But the alternative, to do nothing, was unthinkable.

One sharp word from the teacher and every student slid from his chair, crouched under his desk, and held up a jacket to shield his head from the glass that was already shattering. Kai waited until his teacher had pulled his suit coat over his head. He scrambled silently for the door, snatching his outdoor shoes from the cubby as he went. A shock wave ran along the floor like a ripple on a pond. Lights flickered and went out. Another tremor followed, and a third, and then nothing. Kai ran. He cleared the front door, crossed the play yard, scaled the fence, and headed into town. Tsunami sirens blared a rising note of warning.

Kai sprinted past the turn that led to his parents' apartment. They would be fine at the power plant behind the seawall. Their full attention would be needed at the reactor to keep it running safely. Kai knew where he was needed. He flew down the hill, the last direction anyone would go—toward the curve of shoreline and the small fishing boats moored there.

People streamed out of their homes and headed for high ground. Ocean bottom appeared where the bay should have been. The decaying hull of a boat that

sank years ago sat exposed in the mud. Fish flopped in the unexpected air. Kai spared less than a second to look for the *Ushio-maru* at the marina. He and his grandfather hadn't sailed it in months, not since his grandmother had a stroke. But the *Ushio-maru* was there in the marina as always. It was beached like all the rest of the boats, but Kai knew the ocean would be back, as relentless as a freight train, showing mercy to no living thing.

"Ojī-san! Obā-san!" Kai called as he rounded the corner to his grandparents' house, a block above the harbor. One side of the blue-tile roof was already a heap of rubble burying his grandmother's garden.

He took the wooden steps in a single bound. He found them in the main room of their house, kneeling beneath the futon Ojī-san had pulled from the closet and held as a shield over their heads. Kai slid to his knees.

"You can't stay here."

"Kai, why are you here?" Obā-san reached to cup his face, even as Kai bowed his apology. "You should be taking shelter with your schoolmates at the shrine," Obā-san said. "What will they say if you are not there?"

"Come with me," Kai said.

Another boom sounded from the *ōdaiko* under the earth. The floor lurched forward and back. Cabinet doors swung open, and dishes and cans tumbled out. Daylight showed through cracks in the walls. Books toppled from the shelf. Kai scooted closer to his *obā-san* to shield her. Ojī-san bent the futon over all three of them like a tent. Kai closed his eyes against the dust. When the shaking stopped, Ojī-san lifted the futon and looked at the ruins of his house.

"We should all go to the shrine," Kai said. "It's only two kilometers. Two. I'll carry her. I'm big enough."

Obā-san's walker and the dining table were the only upright objects in the room.

"So far!" Obā-san said. "You go. We'll meet you there."

"Together!" Kai insisted, lowering his head to apologize for his stubbornness but then looking to his grandfather, imploring.

Ojī-san stood up slowly, testing his limbs and the uneven floor. He reached for his wife and helped her stand. He moved to her weaker side, supporting as she found her balance, speaking softly into her ear, to help her find courage.

"Together," Ojī-san said. "We will go as far as we are able."

Kai took his grandmother's other arm, and they made their way across the tilted floor and into the ruined street.

2

THREE MINUTES AND forty-seven seconds later, on the far side of the Pacific, Jet watched her dad bring ships across the Columbia Bar. She sat on her porch roof, binoculars trained on the mouth of the river, resting against the frame of her bedroom window. Afternoon shadows stretched across the yard below. The rough asphalt shingles were worn smooth from the hundreds of times Jet had watched her dad piloting tankers, car carriers, and container ships through the shifting currents and past the mountain of sand that made the entrance into the Columbia River the most dangerous passage in the Pacific. Jet's stereo played the unmusical chatter of marine radio. On her phone she toggled between the day's weather, the ocean's currents, and the local tides.

Her dad was navigating the trickiest part of the passage, the eye of the needle—a narrow spot between Point Adams and the Desdemona Sands. As the container ship drew closer to Astoria, Jet could make out the name on the starboard side, *Hanjin Oslo 952*. She checked the vessel-traffic list. It was a Korean ship bound for Portland: 623 tons of cargo, twenty-one feet of draft. Dad had piloted plenty of boats with a deeper draft; no way he'd run this one aground. She pictured him on the bridge of the *Hanjin Oslo* in his yellow float coat with PILOT written across the shoulder in block letters. The captain would be at his side to translate his directions to the crew.

An alarm sounded on her phone. It was from NOAA—the ocean guys. A tsunami warning flashed across the screen. Jet dropped her binoculars and flicked through the website for details. Quake magnitude: greater than six. Epicenter: a hundred miles from Osaka. Flooding expected on the southern third of Japan in the next twenty minutes. Alerts went up for all the islands in the Pacific and the western coasts of North and South America.

Osaka? Jet tried to remember the name of her cousin's hometown. Wasn't it somewhere in the middle? No,

it was south, definitely south of Osaka. Kai was fine last time, when the quake was in the north. Besides, his town had mountains just like Astoria, plenty of high ground to get away from rising water. Every town on the Oregon coast had evacuation routes for emergency flooding. Jet had more tsunami drills than fire drills at school. No worries there.

But what would her dad do about his ship? Last time there was a quake on the Japan side of the Pacific, it took hours for the high water to get to Astoria. Last time the warning had come to nothing—barely a ripple on the north Oregon coast. But down by the California border, it had crushed whole marinas and stacked the fishing fleet three deep as if the vessels were bathtub toys.

Would Dad close the bar? Would he turn the ship around and make it wait out the tsunami in deep water? A pilot had the authority. He could stop a million dollars' worth of river traffic and delay shipping schedules as far away as Chicago. Or he could make a run for it and get the *Hanjin Oslo* up the Columbia far enough that the surge of a tsunami couldn't touch it.

Jet grabbed her binoculars and gave the *Hanjin Oslo* the most careful examination that three miles of

distance allowed. It was a newer ship, no visible rust or broken equipment. She was fully loaded, but a sliver of red along the side of the ship showed she hadn't exceeded her load water line. Had Dad piloted this ship before? Jet pulled out her log and flipped through it. Yes, ten months ago, so he'd know the captain and the quality of her crew.

The warning came over marine radio. High water in two hours in the Philippines, in four hours on the coast of New Guinea, seven hours for Hawaii and Alaska. He had more than seven hours. Plenty of time to get the ship miles up the river and all three of the tankers moored in the mouth of the Columbia out into the safety of deep water.

Jet stood up, gripping the gutter on the roof above her window and straining for a better view of the ship. She willed herself to see into the bridge. Imagined the array of instruments at his command.

"Come on, Dad, you can make it!" Jet said to nobody.

She watched and waited. When the *Hanjin Oslo* inched its way past the mouth of Youngs Bay and moved into position to go under the Astoria Bridge, Jet pumped a fist in the air just for the satisfaction of knowing she'd made the right call.

3

"RUN!"

Ojī-san's last word echoed in Kai's head as his feet pounded the ground behind the fish cannery, propelling him forward even as his heart called him to turn back.

Kai had thought they were safe. Four floors up should have been safe, but one boat after another had broken loose from the marina and plowed into the old cannery building, breaking through the loading area and collapsing the ocean-facing wall. Most of the cannery workers had fled, but it had taken all their strength to get Obā-san to the cannery and up four flights of stairs. The Ikata Seafood Company was the only tall building on the waterfront. It was concrete and steel. It should hold. And yet the walls shook as if they were made of paper, and the lowest floor was already submerged.

Ojī-san had shown him an escape route, a chute that ran from the second floor to a line of trucks in the loading dock behind the plant. Beyond that was a chain-link fence, the highway, and a hillside too steep for houses.

There was no time to choose or even speak. Kai took the loading chute to the roof of the first truck. He ran the length of the truck's roof and jumped to the one parked behind it, landing with inches to spare. He fell forward, skinning the palms of his hands on a metal seam. The sting barely registered. Water rose up to the belly of the truck. Kai felt it shudder and lift free of the pavement. He staggered the length of the trailer as it swung to the side and crashed into the retaining wall of the freeway. He jumped for the chain-link fence on top of the wall, climbed over, and dropped to the highway. The hill on the other side of the road was so steep he had to go on hands and knees. By the time he reached the top, Kai had exhausted everything but the will to run.

He ran farther than he thought possible, cutting loops off the paved roads that switchbacked up the

hills, plowing through brush and ferns. It was almost dark, and Kai was near the crest of the hills when a final aftershock threw him to the ground.

He stayed where he fell, face in the dirt and heart racing, until long after the earth was still. A rivulet of runoff was only inches away. Kai scooted toward it, lowering his face to lap up water. Eventually the heat of his body and the heat of his fear cooled, leaving him no company but horror and shame.

How could he have run, even to obey? He wasn't a little boy who needed babysitting from his grandparents anymore. All that had changed when Obā-san had her stroke. Now he was the one to help Ojī-san look after her. No more fixing boats down at the marina with his grandfather's friends. No more after-school sails. Kai was there to work in the garden, to shop at the fish market, to make her laugh every day, and to help her learn to walk again. Kai slowly rose to his feet, ache in every inch of him. He looked toward town to see if the fish cannery was still standing.

There was nothing to see but smoke.

Kai knew where he should be. The thought of facing his principal—of explaining why he'd run off instead of following orders and trusting the neighbors to take

care of his grandparents—filled him with dread. He could already hear the things Kōchō-sensei would say.

No. Better not to explain. Better to take his punishment without excuses. But what if his grandparents lived? What if the cannery building held together, and they were out there right now? If he could find them and bring them to safety, no one would question his choice. But what if he never found them? What if he searched the whole town? What if . . .

Kai spun one awful possibility after another as darkness closed in around him. He checked the cuts on his elbows and knees. He cleaned them with spit and the shirttail of his uniform. The wind was as warm as any June breeze, but Kai shivered anyway, curling his body against a cold no coat or blanket could touch.

He spent the night trying not to hear the fires, or smell them. He'd always thought of fire as beautiful, a cheery addition to a summer picnic. But fire, real fire, was loud. The sulfur glow of it miles below didn't so much cast light as deepen the shadows. And the smell of burning cars, burning boats, burning houses—the smell was the hardest to escape.

4

SOME MORNINGS ARE so perfect, it's a crime not to go sailing. The first morning of summer vacation was such a day. Jet knew it the moment she opened her eyes and heard the wind in the cedars. She tugged on last year's swim-team Speedo, a pair of her comfiest boy swim trunks, and a sweatshirt from Rose City Comic Con, where her mom had a book signing last year. She skipped the brush, pulled her sleep-tangled blond hair into a ponytail, and then headed downstairs to snag some breakfast.

Oliver was lounging on the living room floor in his Spider-Man pajamas, already lost in a book. Jet went into the kitchen. Mom was sitting at her computer, glued to the tsunami news with the volume turned down so Oliver wouldn't hear.

It had taken twelve hours to get word from Japan. When the text came through, Dad hollered like the house was on fire. He picked Mom up off the ground and spun her in circles. But then he read the text. Aunt Hanako and Uncle Lars were safe, but Kai was missing and so were his grandparents.

Jet had heard her parents talking long into the night. She had wanted to say something to them, something comforting. But her track record for saying the right thing was not spectacular. She'd hidden in her room instead.

And now she hid behind the fridge door, just as uncertain about what to say to her mom, who looked like she might cry at any moment. She turned her thoughts to the contents of the fridge. The breakfast shakes were too healthy; the yogurt was too pink. Hot dogs sounded good, but Oliver had a habit of licking them and putting them back. She scooped up three muffins and a juice box and headed back to her room. She paused at the foot of the stairs. Her brother was still in the living room, waving an imaginary sword in one hand while he read his way through yet another of Horatio Hornblower's famous sea battles. Typical! If she didn't do something, he'd be there six hours later, no breakfast, still fighting Napoleon. She should get him out of the house for the day, so Mom could stop worrying about the news frightening him. She should take him sailing. That would be better than anything she could say.

"Oliver," Jet said. "Oliver!"

He didn't even hear her.

"Dude!" She threw a muffin straight at his head, landing it solid just above his ear.

"Hey," Oliver said. He rubbed the cinnamon-sugar spot on his hair.

"Eat something. We're sailing in half an hour!"

"But . . . I'm . . ." Oliver waved an arm at the page and searched his highly advanced third-grade vocabulary for a word to express how important this book was to him.

"Bring it along! If we hit a calm, you can read in the boat."

Oliver looked wistfully around the living room. There was a shelf with ten more Horatio Hornblowers on it and another shelf with *Master and Commander* and Sherlock Holmes, plus all of Mom's comic books. Sometimes even laser tag wasn't a good enough bribe to get him out of there.

"Look, it's the first day of summer. Nobody ever died from fresh air, you know!"

"Can't you sail with Beck?" Oliver said. "You like Beck."

Jet sighed. How could she possibly explain? She wasn't even sure herself what had gone wrong. Last summer Beck had been over almost every day for their epic construction project—a tree fort, rock wall, and zip line. Last summer their dads finally let them crew the *Saga* alone. Last summer Roland hadn't moved to town yet.

Jet reached over and brushed a clump of cinnamon sugar from Oliver's buzz-cut red hair.

"Well, I like you better," she said. "So eat something!" Jet pointed to the muffin on the floor. "And milk!" she called over her shoulder as she took the stairs two at a time.

Jet slid the window up and settled into her usual spot on the porch roof. A city crew was almost finished mending the section of the boardwalk that had broken away in the rising water. A tugboat pulled a tsunami-damaged fishing boat from its mooring and towed it away for repair. Jet nodded with satisfaction to see things set right on the waterfront. She

couldn't have done better if she'd been in charge herself.

She opened her juice box. Her cousin Kai's town had taken the worst of the tsunami that followed the earthquake. Just like last time, the power plant was in trouble. Not a meltdown. Not yet. But trouble. Jet had watched the news for an hour, and then she couldn't take it anymore. The rising water was relentless, and nobody had time to prepare. In Astoria they'd had hours. People had time to move their stuff. A friend of Mom's had packed up his entire waterfront studio and put all his paintings and art supplies in their garage just in case. And then the water only rose a dozen feet— enough to break a few boats and flood a few shops and make the riverfront roads muddy. It wasn't fair that they got off so easy and Japan was suffering again.

Jet tried to remember her cousin. He'd come to America with Uncle Lars and Aunt Hanako when she was too little to remember. She'd been to Japan for a visit once, when she was seven and Oliver was tiny. Jet remembered a house with a blue roof, but she couldn't remember a thing about the boy with jet-black hair and freckles, whose school pictures showed up every year on the refrigerator.

She took a few bites of muffin and then grabbed her binoculars. Feathery clouds in the west showed no trace of the storm predicted for later in the day, but the wind was already picking up. Jet tugged her hood up over her head. The pilots were still busy clearing backed-up traffic from the tsunami warning that closed the bar three days ago. People had been finding all kinds of crazy stuff along the shore, now that the high water had passed: boat fenders in the road, gill nets tangled in bushes, harbor seals taking shelter miles upriver. Jet was dying to get out and explore it all.

She wasn't the only one. Lots of kids had their eyes on the water. You had to be twelve to enter the Treasure Island Race, the highlight of the Astoria Regatta and the most hotly contested championship in town. She and Beck had started training for the race together last summer. Beck's dad, Captain Chandler, was a bar pilot too. He and Jet's dad took turns taking her and Beck out in the *Saga,* the same dinghy her dad used when he won the Treasure Island Race with Uncle Lars a zillion years ago. Captain Chandler grew up sailing the Chesapeake in a little boat just like it, and both captains were determined to see their kids be the youngest team ever to win the race. Jet could feel that

championship cup in her hand. She could imagine her picture on the front page of the *Daily Astorian.*

Jet polished off her muffins and licked the cinnamon sugar from her fingers. She picked up her phone and thought about texting Beck for a sail that morning. Beck loved days like this.

Last summer it had been simple. But then came sixth grade, and for the first time since kindergarten Beck didn't sit in Jet's row. He picked a spot clear over on the other side of the room next to Roland, the new kid in town. At lunch there was a girl table and a boy table. Even worse, nobody played soccer or even basketball at recess anymore. The boys stood around and talked about hunting and played video games. Skye and Bridgie and the rest of the girls were all about clothes and music videos. Suddenly headphone sharing was a thing, and everyone was a foot taller than her.

Then the worst thing of all: Captain Chandler missed his jump one stormy night in November. He survived, and that was lucky, but his legs were crushed between the pilot boat and the oil tanker he'd been boarding. He spent almost a month in the hospital in Portland and the rest of the winter learning to use a wheelchair. Beck stopped talking to Jet altogether that

winter. Was he mad at her because her dad was fine and his wasn't? Dad and Captain Chandler were still friends. It didn't make sense. Maybe boys just stopped talking to girls in the sixth grade.

Jet typed out *Sail?* and hit Send. She didn't want a boyfriend. She and Beck didn't even have to be best friends. But why couldn't they be sailing partners?

5

AT SUNRISE KAI set out for the emergency shelter at the shrine. He found a cell-phone tower in a clearing a short distance away. The fence around it looked completely untouched, but the cell-tower mast was tilted like a fishing rod. Kai took out his phone. It had half a battery left but no reception at all. He shut it down. There was no point in keeping it, but he pocketed the phone out of habit.

Kai looked toward the ocean. The water had gone down, and a few of the buildings in town were still standing, but he couldn't see the fish cannery from where he stood. The cannery had survived other earthquakes. His grandparents could be alive. They were far above sea level, on the fourth floor. They could have sheltered overnight and even now be finding a way to safety. Ojī-san had gathered coats and water and Obā-san's medicine on the way out the door. He would find a way to save her.

Kai trudged down the hill, working his way around fallen trees, alert for landslides. As the day grew warmer, hunger and thirst made his head swim, but nothing in the forest looked like food. Just by luck he happened across a nest late in the afternoon. Kai crouched beside it and considered the gray-speckled eggs. They were beautiful in their own plain way. The mama bird, some kind of lark, was scolding him from a tree branch above. Kai could not bring himself to touch those eggs. So much around him was in ruins. It felt wrong to break an egg now. Kai made do with stream water.

It was dark by the time he reached the shrine. The emergency shelter was set up in the open area in front of the offering hall. People packed every available spot. A few kerosene lanterns spread rings of light through the crowd. There would be a procedure, Kai was certain. He looked around for the leader.

"Kai?" a voice called from the shadows. "Is it you?"

"It's him!"

"He's alive!"

Kai turned and was surrounded by Tomo and Hiroshi and some of the other boys from school. They bombarded him with questions about where he'd been. They took him to Kōchō-sensei. The school principal sat at the table, ear pressed to a hand-cranked radio. There was a mud-spattered briefcase beside him, two first-aid kits, and a dozen road flares. A portable radiation detector beeped and displayed a number. Kōchō-sensei copied it in a column on his school ledger. There was a second clipboard with a long list of names.

The boys fell quiet as they came closer, stopping just inside the ring of lamplight. When the principal looked up, they nudged Kai forward.

"It's Ellstrom-kun. We found him," Hiroshi said.

Kai's mouth went dry. He fixed his eyes on a spot of dirt in front of his principal's shoes. The boys shuffled their feet nervously, as if they were somehow to blame for forming a friendship with the kind of person who would be so thoughtless as to run off in a crisis. They searched for something correct to say.

"Are we all accounted for now?" Tomo said.

Kōchō-sensei ignored the boys and turned to Kai. He launched into a lengthy scolding. Kai stood with his head down. He put all his energy into letting the

words roll away from him without sinking in, and they all did, all except one—*hāfu*. Who else would do something so completely disrespectful of the others in the group? When the scolding was done, Kai murmured "thank you" and looked up. Kōchō-sensei dismissed them all with a nod.

Kai hesitated. "My grandparents. Are they . . ."

Kōchō-sensei shook his head. "The tunnels are caved in, the lower parts of the road washed away. Go with your classmates. Rest. I'll need workers in the morning."

Kai followed his classmates past families who had staked a space for themselves. They came to an open place and smoothed out sleeping spots on the ground. Tomo wordlessly invited Kai to scoot in closer and rest his head on the jacket he'd spread out. Gradually the lanterns were put out. The whimpering babies were quieted. The wind shifted, carrying the worst of the smells from the ruined town out to sea.

Kai tried to let sleep come, but it didn't. Eventually he gave up. He walked silently among the sleeping people, pausing whenever he saw gray hair. He pulled out his phone, lit up the screen, and shone it on the faces of the seniors from his town. Some he knew—friends

and fishing companions of his grandparents—but none were the faces he was looking for. He searched silently until he'd used his last drop of battery life.

The moon rose, the sky was clear, and there was enough light to see the road. Kai glanced around to be sure no one was watching. One man sat at Kōchō-sensei's table beside the emergency radio, his eyes fixed on the radiation counter. Kai headed down the road, walking as quietly as he could, listening for movement. A cry for help. Anything.

The air was still, and it was unearthly quiet, as if every mouse and bird had vanished. He came to a bend in the road, and in the moonlight he could see the ocean. Smoke drifted over the water, and there were a few scattered lights of deep yellow and orange.

Obā-san had a favorite story about ghostly lights that hovered over the water where men had lost their lives at sea. But these were no ghost lights. These were real ships, and they were on fire.

Kai shuddered and turned away from the water. He was so rattled that he almost didn't see the wash-out in the road until it was too late. He gasped as the curve of wet pavement appeared in the moonlight only a few feet ahead. Beyond the high-water mark was the

jagged ring of asphalt where the tsunami had taken a monster-size bite out of the road. Broken slabs of pavement, highway railing, and shattered trees littered the ground fifty feet below. The gap left behind was as large as a baseball diamond. There was no way across. Not for an old man leading a woman who could barely walk.

But Ojī-san was the smartest, bravest man Kai knew. He'd never give up. Never.

Kai swallowed back tears, crammed his hands into his pockets, and closed a fist around his phone. Without thinking, he took it out and hurled it as hard as he could at the ocean.

6

KAI WOKE IN the morning, cold and damp. He shook the dew from his hair and brushed it off his uniform jacket. He braced himself against shivering and against thoughts about his grandparents. He joined his classmates in the line for food and water. Kōchō-sensei's steady voice was calling out directions. There was only a mouthful of peanuts and a morsel of dried fish.

Kai looked at the stack of emergency rations and the size of the crowd. The supplies wouldn't last long, maybe not even past tomorrow. There were *mikan* farms in the hills, but the oranges wouldn't be ripe for months. Kai licked the last of the salt from his fingers. With the roads washed out, they'd have to do something to find more food.

After breakfast as they were breaking into work groups, a foghorn rang out in three short blasts and a long one. A fishing boat appeared on the horizon. It was the green-and-red trawler that belonged to the son of Ojī-san's best friend. Kai let out a roar. He threw an arm around Tomo's shoulder and pounded him on the back. The rest were jumping and shouting.

"They made it!" Kai shouted. "They're alive!"

"They've got fish!" Hiroshi yelled.

Kai could just make out the red flag a fishing boat flew when it was making its way toward the cannery.

"We should help carry the catch up," Kai said. There was wood in the forest for fires. Fish could be roasted on sticks. A full boat would feed them all. The boys gathered around him and worked out a plan.

Kōchō-sensei beamed when they brought him the news of the fish and their plan to bring it to the shelter. He pulled a group together to meet the fishing boat. In a few minutes Kai was following a dozen men and older boys into town.

As they came out of the hills, Kai heard the hum of small powerboats. When they stopped at an over-look to scout for a safe path into town, they could see a few small boats picking their way along the shore. One

was pulling a family from the roof of a house. Another called out for survivors with a bullhorn.

Hope sprang up in Kai like a struck match. His grandparents could be alive! The front half of the cannery building lay in ruins, but there was a section still standing. He looked for a route that would take them closer, but the whole waterfront was a jumble of mud and debris. Upended cars and boats lay side by side in the wreckage. When the team arrived at the harbor, Kai questioned the huddled group of survivors. No one had seen his grandparents.

"Plenty yet to find," one of the rescuers said.

"We'll do our best," his partner added. "There's a boat taking some to the hospital in Matsuyama. Ask them."

The men in the group were deep in conversation with another rescue team about how to safely bring the catch of fish ashore. Kai and the other boys stood together, waiting for their moment to be helpful. A larger boat landed.

"Ellstrom!" a man's voice trumpeted out.

"Kai Ellstrom!" shouted another.

Kai turned toward the voices, knowing them even before they came into sight. Miller and Valdez were

navy veterans, friends of his dad's, from the next island over. They'd been retired as long as Kai had known them, but they still did odd jobs for fishermen and a ton of local search and rescue. They'd both been corpsmen.

"Hah! Found him!" Miller strode across the broken pavement and pounded Kai on the back. He turned to Valdez. "Ya owe me a beer!"

"Hey, man." Valdez held out a hand to shake but then thumped Kai on the back anyway. "Promised Ellstrom we'd find you."

"You talked to my dad?"

"Oh-dark-early this morning," Miller said. "We're doing the hospital runs." He pointed to their boat. A hugely pregnant woman sat in the stern. She was holding an IV bag for a man who was lying down. "The power plant was on our way."

"Is everybody . . ." Kai suddenly ran out of breath. He'd been sure his mom and dad were safe. The power plant had more emergency supplies than anyone. But what if . . .

"They're fine," Valdez said quickly. "Every single one."

"We need to talk to whoever's in charge over here," Miller said.

Kai led his father's friends to the group.

"Konnichiwa," Miller began with a bow. He explained that he was there to take the survivors most critically hurt to the nearest hospital. They had room for six more on this run. He said that the coast guard, with their water and food, were at least another day away, maybe two. And then he lowered his voice and started talking urgently about the power plant.

"What's going on?" Kai said. "Is something wrong at the plant?" Ever since the last earthquake, one safety measure after another had been put in place.

Valdez shifted his stance a bit. "Not yet," he said.

"Yet?" Kai felt a chill run the length of his body. Hiroshima was only 150 kilometers away. Radiation poisoning and the atomic bomb were things he studied every year in school.

"Many things are broken," Valdez said quietly. "Every single one of them is fixable. But just in case, they sent along some extra radiation counters."

Kai and Valdez brought three boxes of them from the boat to where the men were discussing radiation and clean drinking water with Miller. Valdez moved on to the other survivors with a medical kit in hand.

"One more thing," Miller said. He drew a letter out

of his shirt pocket. "We're taking Lars and Hanako's son with us." He handed over the letter. "His folks are going to be working around the clock for weeks, and he's got family to stay with in America."

"What?" Kai gasped. "But I have a job. We're bringing fish up for people to eat."

The men in the group moved back to the work of unloading fish, but not before giving Kai stern looks for his undignified outburst. Miller lowered his voice and switched to English. "Look around you, Kai. There's no clean water, no food, no power, no phones. Things are going to get a whole lot worse before they get better."

"More reason to stay and help," Kai insisted.

"One less mouth to feed. One less kid to keep track of."

"I'm not a kid. I'm working."

Miller sighed and leaned closer, so they were speaking almost in a whisper. "The hard part hasn't even started yet. People are pulling together fine today, and they'll be fine tomorrow, but a week from now, when everyone is hot and hungry, when people start getting sick, and they still don't have a roof over their heads, and the power is still out . . ."

Miller paused. He looked around the ruins of the town.

"If your folks were here, right here with you, it would be different," he went on. "But this is no place for a kid to be on his own."

Kai balled his hands into fists. "This is my home! I won't run away!"

Miller crossed his well-muscled and heavily tattooed arms over his chest. He was the only person Kai had ever met who was as tall as his dad. They were almost the only grown-ups left who towered over him.

"I promised your father I'd bring you to the airport, and I will, even if I have to tie you up in a sack to get you there."

"A little help here?" Valdez barged in. He was serving as a crutch for a woman who had a row of bloody gashes below her knee. Kai went to the woman's other side. His anger was still bubbling, but he fell in step with the injured woman and helped Valdez get her into the boat.

"That kid who's wheezing," Valdez said over his shoulder. "Might be a respiratory thing."

Kai scurried back to help Valdez with his next casualty and the one after that.

34

"I could stay with you," Kai said quietly as they helped the last injured man into the boat. "I'll work hard. I'll do whatever you say. I'm not afraid of anything. Please."

Miller sighed. "I don't doubt you, Kai. But I gave Ellstrom my word. Are you going to make a liar of me?"

Miller's job in the navy was probably anchor. He was solid as a tree. And he was definitely not kidding about tying Kai up in a sack. It was only the prospect of being scooped up and carried away like a toddler that made Kai get into the boat with as much dignity as he could muster.

As his hometown grew smaller in the distance, Kai felt shame wash over him. He'd failed at everything he'd tried, and now there was no way to make it up. He'd be the coward who ran away. Forever. He tried to bear it as Ojī-san would want him to, but a groan that he could not hold in escaped.

7

JET CHECKED HER phone one last time. Beck hadn't returned her text. Not that she cared. No. Sailing with her little brother was just fine.

"Ten minutes!" she hollered to Oliver.

He was reading in exactly the same position on the living room floor, as if time had stood still. Jet got a glass of milk, a plate, and a banana from the kitchen. She retrieved his muffin from the floor, confiscated the book, and nudged him toward the food.

"No breakfast, no book, mister," she said firmly.

Oliver glared at her, crammed the whole muffin in his mouth, and chewed with his mouth open. He held out his hand for the book. A cascade of blueberry crumbs fell to the rug. Jet shuddered, returned the book, and retreated to the kitchen. She filled a plastic bag with M&M's and mini-marshmallows. The morning paper wasn't on the table. Never mind. She could see the weather was fine; she'd get the tide later.

The streets were quiet when Jet and Oliver flew down the hill on their bikes. They took a left at the highway and turned off when they came to the sailing club.

It was nothing fancy. In Astoria, sailors were fishermen, cannery workers, and loggers. They patched up old pleasure boats or repurposed worn-out fishing dories. The club had a mossy boat ramp, a dock, a few picnic tables, and a row of sheds where people could store their boats in the winter. A bulletin board had flyers for the regatta, a thing about the Regatta Princess Pageant, boats for sale, and a tattered sheet of paper with the tide table.

Jet ignored it all, except for the tide table. She ran her finger down the date column. The table stopped with the last day of May. Jet got out her phone and punched her tides app. It loaded at a snail's pace.

"Did you get the tide this morning?" she asked. Oliver shrugged and leaned his bike up against Jet's. "We should check. Dad would murder me if I forgot something so basic as check the tide."

"Don't worry about it," Oliver said.

He took the bag of treats and walked onto the dock where the *Saga* was tied up. He fished a handful of marshmallows out of the bag and threw them into Youngs Bay. For a moment they just bobbed in the water, but then they started moving toward the Columbia River and out to sea.

"The tide's going out," Oliver announced.

Jet shook her head and smiled. Oliver had been reading before kindergarten, and he remembered everything. Dad had showed them the marshmallow trick three summers ago.

"Rats!" Jet said.

They weren't supposed to sail on an outgoing tide. The shipping lane lay across the mouth of Youngs Bay. It was no place for a sailboat as small as theirs. A seagull swooped in and ate a marshmallow.

"It's not going very fast," Oliver said.

More seagulls came and squawked over the remaining marshmallows. Jet looked at their beloved *Saga*. She was tiny, barely twelve feet from bow to stern, oars instead of a motor, nothing fancy about her. But Jet loved her clean lines and sky-blue decks. The boat had been in her family since Dad was a kid. Sometimes

they looked around on the sailboat websites for something new, but Jet knew her dad would never part with the boat that won him the championship.

"The tide's probably about to turn," Oliver said.

Early-morning sunlight shimmered on the mudflats around the edges of the bay. The old pilings were sticking up more than six feet above the water. It was as low a tide as she'd ever seen.

"Yeah," Jet said. "But we should wait. Just to be safe."

Oliver took out his book and dove headlong into naval warfare while Jet leaned back to soak up the sun. After nine months of rain, it was easy to forget how quickly her skin went from winter white to summer lobster. Jet was slathering on sunscreen when she heard a truck coming down the drive. It was Captain Chandler's van, the new one with the wheelchair lift. Maybe Beck wanted to sail with her, after all.

The van pulled into the drive, and Jet caught sight of a boat trailer. She stood on tiptoes for a better view. It looked like a Hobie, one of those racing boats that had two hulls and a trampoline deck. They weren't the kind of all-purpose boat the *Saga* was, with room enough for camping gear or fishing tackle or little brothers.

Nope, a Hobie did one thing. It went fast—really fast! The van rolled to a stop, and before Jet could even take a step in their direction, the side door slid open, and Beck popped out. Roland was right behind him.

Jet turned away. She should go up there and chat with them about the new boat. That's what her dad would do. She and Beck had been friends since they were tiny. It was silly not to. But everything about Roland rubbed her the wrong way. It's not just that he was so competitive. She didn't mind having someone to push her at swim team, although, to be perfectly honest, she was a little steamed when he won the Geography Bee last month. No, what she minded was that he was a dork to girls. Separate tables at lunch was his idea.

"Come on, Oliver," Jet said. "Let's get out there."

8

OLIVER TOOK HIS usual spot at the bow of the *Saga*. Jet tossed him a life jacket and slipped into her own. She swung the front of the boat away from the dock and hopped into the stern. The wind was steady from the east. Jet lowered the rudder into the water. Oliver raised the mainsail and then the jib. Jet settled herself comfortably in the stern of the boat with the mainsheet in her right hand. She felt the familiar thrill as she took the tiller in her left to steer the boat. Her grandfather's initials were carved into the polished mahogany of the tiller handle. Her father and Uncle Lars had their initials carved beside his. Last August, after Jet's first solo sail, Dad carved her initials right beside his. Beck made his first solo the same day, and they had a big barbecue at the Chandlers' place to celebrate.

Winning the Treasure Island Race was the first step on her path. All the bar pilots had been kid sailors, and every one of them had regatta trophies. Jet knew it would take plenty of work to go from sailing a twelve-foot dinghy to piloting a thousand-foot Panamax cargo ship. But from here on out, it was all practice. Jet felt her heart soar as wind filled the sails and pushed them across the water. In a boat it didn't matter that she was the shortest kid in her class. Seamanship was all that counted. She pulled in the mainsheet to adjust the sail, getting a feel for the strength of the wind and the tug of the current.

The rivers that dumped into Youngs Bay were tiny compared to the Columbia, and usually Youngs Bay was flat and easy—not quite a lake, but the safest open water for miles around. Jet pulled the tiller toward her to swing the nose of the *Saga* upstream and away from the shipping lane. The wind dumped out of her sail, and they came to a standstill.

"We're going to have to beat windward," Jet said. "Are we clear on your side?"

"All clear," Oliver answered.

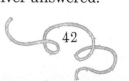

"Perfect," Jet said. "Ready about?"

"Ready."

"Helm's alee."

She slid the tiller away from her and let the boom swing out over the starboard rail.

"Duck!" Jet called.

She grabbed her brother's head and pulled it down so the metal bar holding the bottom of the sail wouldn't hit him. They fell into a rhythm of tacking back and forth, Jet manning the mainsail and Oliver handling the smaller jib in the front of the boat. Jet didn't look back at the sailing-club dock.

Except every once in a while.

The new boat was longer than the *Saga,* maybe four or five feet longer.

She chatted naval strategy with Oliver. She listened to his idea for the perfect pirate movie.

The new boat had a red sail. It was named the *Viking.*

"Kind of weird that we haven't gotten any farther, isn't it?" Oliver said.

They'd been zigzagging for twenty minutes and still hadn't gotten past Dagget Point.

"The tide must still be going out," Jet said. She took

another hard look at the shore on either side of them. "Weird, though, because the tide is already super low."

"I'm bored. Let's go home," Oliver said.

The new boat was rigged up and ready. No way was Jet going back there where Roland could mock her with a bigger boat.

"Let's stay a little longer," she said to Oliver. "We can go toward the mouth of the bay, where there's more room to run. It'll be lots more fun."

"What about the tide?"

"Let's check." Jet held the mainsheet in her teeth, fished her phone out of her pocket, and handed it off to her brother. Oliver ran his finger along the screen, scrolling through icons.

"Here it is." Oliver tapped the screen and then frowned. "It says we're at high tide. That's messed up. Is this a free app?"

"No way. Let me see."

Oliver leaned toward the stern, holding the phone out for her to look.

"Well, duh! That's for Hawaii."

The trouble with the phone tide table was that you needed a hand free to use it. If Beck were here she'd

just hand him the tiller and mainsheet, but Oliver wasn't big enough for that.

"Ready about?"

Oliver put the phone away and got ready to turn the boat.

"Helm's alee!"

Jet swung the tiller and let out the mainsheet. A gust of wind caught the sail and swung it across the deck twice as fast as the last time. The *Saga* dipped away from the wind, and Oliver remembered to duck in time to keep the boom from whacking him in the head.

"Mutiny, is it?" Oliver said. "Are you trying to knock me overboard? You pirate!"

He and Dad had just finished their third reading of *Treasure Island*.

"Total mutiny," Jet said. "I was going to maroon you on Haven Island, steal the *Saga,* and head for . . . um . . ."

"Hanapepe Bay?" Oliver said, looking at the phone. "On Kauai, where it's high tide right now. In case you were wondering." He tugged the jib sail over to the same side as the mainsail.

The wind blew harder, making the sails rattle, almost as if the boat was as eager as Jet to go skimming over the water at top speed. Jet looked over her shoulder at the stretch of open water near the bridge. The wind was too perfect to resist.

9

Jet TURNED THE *Saga*'s tail to the wind and her nose to the Columbia. She eased out the mainsheet so the wind filled the mainsail like a big pregnant belly. She felt the *Saga* surge forward.

"Wahoo!" Oliver shouted, leaning over the starboard rail to counterbalance the tilt of the boat.

Jet grinned. The *Saga* was going fast enough to make a real wake, like a powerboat. She let out a whoop of joy. She teased the mainsheet in and out a little to wring every last bit of speed from the wind. She heard the whop-whop of a helicopter. It had the yellow tail with PILOT in black letters on both sides. It was headed out to sea, where a ship was waiting to be guided over the bar.

Oliver laughed and drummed on the hull of the

boat, his boredom forgotten. Jet edged out the tiller to gain speed. Who says an old boat is slow? Handle her right, and the *Saga*'s as fast as any brand-new catamaran. Let Roland and Beck have their shiny new sailboat. It would be all the sweeter when she won the race.

Jet leaned out and looked under the Highway 101 bridge to the Columbia River. A cruise ship was inbound. Jet could see the gleaming white prow of the *Norwegian Jewel,* as tall as any car carrier, bigger than everything except the Panamax container ships, and far cleaner and fancier than anything that carried cargo. She had cleared her turn at Tansy Point, and her pilot would be looking for river traffic, not a tiny sailboat that had no business in those waters. By the time they saw the *Saga,* there'd be no room to stop.

"Shouldn't we turn back?" Oliver called.

"In a minute," Jet answered. She and Dad had a deal about not passing under the bridge.

"Okay! Ready about!" Jet called at the last moment. She wound the mainsheet around her hand twice to be sure she wouldn't lose her grip. She couldn't remember a stronger following wind than this. Ever.

"Helm's alee," Jet said, turning away from the bridge.

Instead of sailing across the wind, the *Saga* slid sideways toward the bridge. Jet could feel water pressing against the blade of the tiller. She had to fight to hold their position. The wind died off for just a moment, and the current swung them back toward the shipping channel.

"Jet?!"

"I know!"

"What's going on?"

"It's the current; it's never been this strong!"

Jet had never sailed this close to the bridge before. Maybe the current was always this strong here. The channel was deep down the middle of the bay. They should never have come this far. Jet pulled the tiller in and turned the nose of the *Saga* toward shore again. Oliver crouched in the bow, a hand on each end of the jib sheet and an eye on the concrete legs of the bridge, which were coming up with alarming speed.

"Jet! Get us out of here!" Oliver yelled.

"Steady," Jet said, more to herself than to her brother.

49

They were gaining the shore, but the outgoing current was so strong, they weren't going to make it before they were swept under the bridge and into the shipping channel. Sweat ran down Jet's back.

The ruins of an abandoned fish cannery stood on the shore just ahead. It was a dangerous spot, with submerged bits of foundation, the rusting remains of a boiler, and rotting pilings sticking out of the water. It was death for a boat in there. But if she could just get close enough, maybe she could get a rope around one of the pilings and hold the *Saga* until the tide came up.

"Oliver," Jet called. "Dig out the anchor."

"It's too deep for the anchor!"

"I'm not going to drop it. I'm going to use it like a lasso."

"You're crazy!" Oliver yelled.

"Not if this works."

Jet took the anchor from him and prayed it would. It was a torpedo-shaped piece of steel, half a foot long, with four arms that folded out. It was about as heavy as a half gallon of milk and tied to a length of red-and-white rope. Jet tied the end of the anchor's rope to the thwart that ran across the middle of the boat.

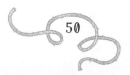

"Get ready to strike the sail," Jet said. "I'm going to need some room to throw."

She looked at the cluster of pilings ahead. There was no way this would work. She'd never tried to rope anything in her life.

"Now!" Jet called. "Drop the sail!"

Oliver untied the halyard and reached up to tug the sail down until it was resting in long folds over the boom.

"Take the tiller," Jet said.

"But I can't steer!"

"Just keep it in the middle. You can do it!"

She put the tiller in his hand. They were out of the swiftest current and over shallow water now, but the tide was still pulling them toward the bridge. Jet stood up, circled the rope and anchor over her head, and let go. The anchor caught in the notch at the top of a wooden piling.

"Yes!" Oliver shouted.

The rope slid through Jet's hands, leaving a red mark. It was a good thing she'd thought to tie off the rope. It grew taut with a snap and yanked the tiller out of Oliver's hand. Jet toppled backward.

51

Oliver pulled Jet back into the helmsman's spot. "Look!" he said. "There's a bunch of stuff down there!"

It was too late. The *Saga*'s hull scraped cement as it passed over a piece of cannery foundation. Jet winced. Oliver clung to the mast, his eyes squeezed shut. Jet tugged an oar out of the oarlock and stood poised to push them away from danger. She saw the rusted remains of the boiler. She stuck the paddle in the water to guide them around it. The oar hit one of the pipes on the boiler, releasing a swirl of scum that hid the rest of the wreckage from sight. There was nothing to do but hold on.

A second later a boiler pipe punched a hole in the side of the *Saga* below the waterline. It felt as if the jagged piece of steel went straight through her heart. Jet forced herself not to scream and scare her brother even more.

"It's okay. We're going to be okay," Jet said firmly, as if saying so could make it true.

Oliver opened his eyes. "We're sinking!"

He was an inch away from screaming, and Jet felt the cold hand of dread pushing her toward panic. She felt the urge to drop everything and hug her little brother until he stopped shaking—her only brother.

How could she have done this? A rookie mistake. Whatever a bar pilot put on his résumé, Jet was pretty sure "zero ships sunk under your command" was the most important thing.

She pulled herself together and looked over the side at the damage. It wasn't as bad as she thought. She took a deep breath and put on a captain's voice. "It's going to be okay," she said. "The split isn't very big."

"Okay," Oliver said. "Now what?"

"Now we wait for the tide."

Jet gave the line a tug to make sure it was secure, then checked the phone. The tide app took a while to load. When it finally pulled up the correct chart, it showed still another half hour until the turn of the tide. Jet buried her head in her hands. How could she have not checked the tide? She always checked the tide. It was in the newspaper. On her phone. In her dad's desk. She'd been in such a hurry. For what? Her dad was going to kill her. What on earth would she say to him? There was just no excuse.

"Snack?" Oliver said, holding out the bag of marshmallows and M&M's.

Jet shook her head. She was never going to eat again. Oliver munched for a while, then took out his

book. When the tide rose, Jet rowed to the edge of the bay. There was water in the buoyancy space behind the hole. Jet scrubbed the area around the split dry and covered it with two layers of duct tape. She pushed the *Saga* back out into the bay. The patch held. She and her brother waded along the mudflats at the edge of the bay, towing the *Saga* in defeat all the way back to its mooring spot. When they rounded the last bend before the sailing club, they saw Beck and Roland launching their brand-new boat on the incoming tide.

10

JET WOKE UP on the couch the next morning, still in her clothes from the night before. In the middle of dinner—finally—they'd gotten the word. Kai was safe! And he needed a place to stay while Uncle Lars and Aunt Hanako were repairing the power plant. Dad had been on the phone past midnight. Apparently sending a kid to another country when his passport is at the bottom of the ocean is a problem. You'd think Kai was a terrorist or something. Lucky that he had dual citizenship, or Dad would probably still be on the phone, yelling at people.

So instead of reciting her carefully rehearsed apology about wrecking the *Saga,* Jet spent most of the night helping move Mom's art stuff from the studio next to Jet's bedroom to the living room, downstairs. A neighbor loaned them a bed. Jet moved her clothes into boxes and gave up her dresser. Mom was in a frenzy of nervous cleaning, almost coming to tears over the ink stains in the carpet. Oliver wandered in bleary-eyed in his pajamas and told Mom to move the bed over the ink spots, making him the hero of the night, even though he'd hardly done any work.

Jet yawned and stretched. She took in the unfamiliar landscape of the living room. The TV and couch were squashed into one corner. Mom's work desk and office chair were crammed in by the window, and her project board, bins of paper, bottles of ink, file cabinet, and cup of five thousand pens squeezed in wherever they fit. Only the fireplace and its row of family pictures remained the same. The house was unnaturally quiet.

Jet wandered into the kitchen and scooped up a well-deserved breakfast of strawberries and ice cream. Notes on the fridge announced which ship Dad was piloting and which flight in Portland Mom was meeting. They'd both be gone for hours.

Oliver came downstairs, poured himself a bowl of

cereal, and picked at it with all the speed and enthusiasm of a banana slug. Oliver did not like strangers. Mom reminded him last night that he and Kai had been buddies when the family visited Japan five years ago. Oliver went to the computer, looked up a child-development website, and announced that "children do not remember things before they are three years old!" It was not the highlight of Mom's evening. And now Oliver was just sitting there. He wasn't even reading the cereal box.

"Park today," Jet announced.

Oliver made his usual grumbles. Jet made her usual promise about stopping at the library on the way home. While he was changing out of pajamas, Jet looked up boat repair on her phone.

"Fiberglass cloth and a can of resin," she mumbled to herself.

Jet fiddled with the repair diagram to enlarge it. The work didn't look super tricky. She'd never fixed a boat on her own, but maybe she could make the repairs without telling Dad about her colossal failure. Conversation with him was not for sissies. He was always loud, and he was always right. Jet had gone over what

she'd say in her head twenty times already, and each time it was more awful. It would be way better if he never found out.

When Oliver was finally done changing, they hopped on their bikes and headed down to the park. Oliver's friends were deeply engaged in an epic jungle-gym war. Jet was relieved to see her brother get swept up in the violence. Her crowd from school was at the park, too, and Roland was in the thick of them like always. He and Beck and the Mikes were practicing jumps in the skate park. Bridgie and Skye were sitting on the swings, cooing over the boys' skateboard tricks and planning their next road trip to the mall in Portland.

Jet went over and sat with them, but her heart wasn't in it. The mall bored her to death. She offered to get them passes to Rose City Comic Con when her Mom went at the end of summer, but only got a luke-warm response. The three of them used to love to go to the kid zone and draw monsters all day long and come home with stacks of free comics and rub-on tattoos. Now Bridgie and Skye were more interested in which movie stars were coming.

It was going to be a long summer.

Biking home took forever. Oliver had a one-speed, and they lived on top of the tallest hill in town. He had to walk it on the steepest part. Jet shifted her bike down to a crawling gear and rode alongside him. They got home just as Mom pulled up.

Her cousin stepped out of the van. No suitcase, no backpack, just a kid in a grass-stained shirt and torn pants. He stood in the vulture position a boy takes when he's in danger of being jumped for his lunch money: shoulders up, chin down. Mom was saying something about the history of the house and the five generations of Ellstroms who'd lived here. Kai nodded as if he was paying attention, but Jet could see the words sheeting off him like rain. Mom had probably been talking all the way from the airport.

"Kai?" Jet said.

"Are you Bridget?"

"Everybody calls me Jet."

In the picture on the fireplace, Kai was five, wearing a kimono and standing outside a temple with a curving red roof. Blond, broad-shouldered Uncle Lars beamed on one side of him, and elegant Aunt Hanako smiled serenely on the other. There was a row of six photos of Kai in his school uniform on the fridge. This

tall rumpled person couldn't possibly be the same boy. He looked so much older.

Jet wracked her brains for something to say. The usual conversation beginners—"How are you? How was your trip?"—seemed wrong. He didn't want to answer those questions. It would be mean to make him answer. Mom seemed intent on carrying the entire conversation, anyway.

"Lunch?" Jet said when her mom paused to draw a breath.

Kai nodded.

"Of course!" Mom said. "You'll be hungry. Let's see . . . peanut butter? Tuna? Ham?" She launched into the full list of sandwich choices.

Jet led them to the kitchen. Kai slid into a chair, folded his hands politely, and fell to blinking and nodding as if his aunt were giving an algebra lesson. Jet consulted her mental map of the Pacific. She counted time zones. No, that couldn't be right.

"What time is it at home?" she whispered while her mother's back was turned.

Kai closed his eyes; he tapped out the numbers on his fingers. "Seven a.m. tomorrow," he said.

"Tomorrow?! Are you kidding?"

Kai shook his head, looking more exhausted by the minute.

"You've been traveling for sixteen hours?" Jet said quietly, still wrapping her head around the dateline Kai had crossed.

Mom had a sandwich in front of him in record time. She turned back to the fridge for milk, still talking. Jet slid the plate to the far side of the table and put a chair cushion in its place. She put one finger between Kai's shoulder blades and pushed him forward. He collapsed onto the table like a dead man. Mom turned around, glass of milk in hand.

"Oh dear," she said.

Kai made a little snore.

"Mom," Jet said firmly. "This boy smells like a gym sock."

"Bridget Jane!"

"Did you get him any clothes? Deodorant? You know, boy stuff?"

Mom leaned on the pantry door. She looked like she hadn't slept in days. "We didn't know what size," she began. "And it took so much longer than I thought it would to clear out my studio and make it a bedroom. And I'm not even finished—"

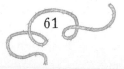

"It's fine," Jet barged in. "You know his size now."

Mom sighed. "You're right. I should pick up a few things."

"The room is perfect," Jet said soothingly.

"Do you think? Maybe he'll want that one up in the attic. It's bigger."

"Oliver lost a frog in the attic two months ago."

"What?!"

"There's the ghost of a dried-up frog up there. Sorry."

Mom shuddered. She could write a whole comic-book series about the zombie apocalypse, but she couldn't cope with amphibians in the house. There was no understanding her.

"Mom," Jet said patiently. "The room is awesome. Kai. Needs. Clothes." She started moving toward the front hall, where Mom had left her purse. "Pajamas? Toothbrush?" Jet kept walking. Mom was not following her. "Starbucks is on the way!" Jet added in her most chipper voice.

Mom looked over her shoulder at Kai. "Poor baby. Alone in the world."

"I'll take care of things here. Kai's asleep. Oliver's reading. What could happen?"

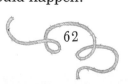

Mom gave her a look. Things had been known to happen on Jet's watch.

"What!" Jet held up both hands. "Oliver is completely frog-free! I checked his pockets. Go!"

Mom laughed. Finally.

"Okay, I'm out of here." She stroked the hair in Jet's ponytail, immediately lodging her fingers in the largest tangle. "Thanks, Jet." She shook her hand free of the tangles and headed out the door. "Just call if—"

"The zombie apocalypse comes this way?"

Mom glared.

"Kidding!" Jet waved and grinned. She restrained herself from slamming the front door, but slumped against it after her mother left. Parents. So exhausting.

Oliver was hiding out with a book in the tree house. Kai wasn't going to wake up for hours, maybe not for several days, so Jet made herself a sandwich and took off for the barn, where her dad kept his office. She settled into his chair. Much as she liked the idea of fixing the boat on the sly, she knew she'd never get away with it, not for long. Dad was loud and goofy, but he wasn't stupid. He'd figure it out. And then what would she say?

There was no excuse. No matter how many times

she ran over the events of the wreck, she couldn't justify it. Forgot to check the tide? Pathetic. Misread the chart? Inexcusable. And a lie. She knew. And she sailed anyway. Would she put up with this kind of incompetence if she were captain? Not a chance.

When he discovered the truth, he'd never let her sail again.

11

HOURS LATER, KAI woke with a start. He glanced around the room, amazed. He remembered where he was. Sixteen hours on a plane was hard to forget, even when you wanted to. It was just that Aunt Karin's kitchen was the largest room he'd ever seen. He slid out of the chair and turned in a full circle. It was a national park of a kitchen, but instead of mountains and forests, it was a trackless landscape of green linoleum, silver appliances, and white countertops. Kai peeked in a cupboard. An army of cans and boxes stood in rank and file, enough to feed a family for a year.

Kai went outside. The yard was empty. He had another cousin, a boy. There were always two of them in the pictures. Storm clouds bruised the sky, hurried by a wind that raised goose bumps on his bare arms. There was an archery target set up at one end of the yard. Two spreading oaks had a zip line between them. A tire swing dangled from one tree, a knotted rope from the other. There wasn't another house in sight.

Kai saw the tail end of the knotted rope disappear up in the branches of the oak tree. Now that he knew where to look, he could see the outline of a tree house, painted with leaves to hide it from view.

Ah, Kai thought. Cousin number two. Oliver, that was his name. He was younger than the girl. Maybe he was afraid of strangers. Maybe he didn't want to share his room. Kai moved away from the tree house to give his cousin some time to get used to the idea of him. From the edge of the yard, Kai could see the river. He felt a twinge in his stomach at the sight.

He pushed his memories of the tsunami aside and instead calculated the distance from the water. Was he more than a thousand meters up? Yes. Easily. Where was higher ground? He glanced all around. This was the high ground.

When they were taking Kai away from home, Miller and Valdez had stopped for a few minutes at the power plant. Instead of saying good-bye to his mother, instead of hugging his father, he'd pleaded to stay with

his friends and help out like everyone else. Before, when his father had proposed sending him to America for the summer, Kai could count on his mother to argue that he should stay and spend his summer preparing for exams at cram school like all the other kids in town. But this time his parents were on the same side.

"How will I face my friends?" he'd said to them. "I'm the only one who's running away from hardship. I'll be ashamed of this forever!"

And then she'd cried. He'd made his mother cry. As if all the rest wasn't bad enough.

"Kai," she'd said. "You are all we have now. You must let your father put you on the highest ground he knows."

Kai turned back now and gave his cousins' house another look. It had once been his father's childhood home, and it did seem to fit him. People were always teasing his father about being tall. He was the wrong size for everybody's furniture. They ordered his lab coats and hazmat suits specially at work. But here he would fit right in.

Kai was already taller than his mom. He had always been the tallest boy in his class. Sometimes when they

were all standing in line at school, Kai would hunch down until he was level with Tomo and Hiroshi and the rest of them. It was rude to stand out against the group. The freckles and the wrong shape of eyes he couldn't fix, but he could pretend not to be tall.

Kai looked along the river, past the bridge, and out to sea. The clouds had gone from iron gray to jet black and the wind was getting steadily stronger. His friends were an ocean away, and there was nothing he could do to fix it. He lifted his head to the wind, feeling the first drops of rain. There had to be some honorable thing he could do while he was here—an honorable American thing. Kai had no idea what it would be.

The drizzle turned to a shower. Kai took shelter under the oak tree. Most June showers in his town were short, but this one got steadily worse. The trees started to sway, and a muffled squeak of alarm came from the tree house overhead. Kai looked up, but Oliver still wasn't showing himself.

Kai headed for the back porch so he wouldn't block Oliver's escape. No sooner had he shut the door than the knotted rope dropped from the tree and a skinny redhead squirreled down it. Oliver sprinted around to the front of the house and ducked inside. Kai heard

a big sigh of relief and the scamper of bare feet going upstairs.

Aunt Karin was waiting for him in the kitchen. She handed him a bag of clothes and showed him where to shower. Kai had been dirty so long, he'd forgotten how bad he smelled. He bowed his thanks and surrendered to the bliss of hot water.

Afterward, he stepped into the living room. He could hear Aunt Karin and his cousins in the kitchen, but he wasn't ready to face them yet. Rain pelted the window, and Kai turned on the lamp by the sofa. Above the fireplace was a row of black-and-white photographs with stern-faced women wearing bonnets and bearded men in uniforms. The pictures got newer toward the end of the row. A man in an army uniform from the Second World War was right beside one of his father in a navy uniform. He'd heard his father talk about some of these people: Grandpa Lars, whom he'd been named for, and Ivar, who'd piloted the bar a hundred years ago. Kai had never seen the pictures before.

It wasn't exactly a shrine, like his grandmother kept. No one would put the picture of a living person in a shrine. There was no trace of burned incense. In fact there wasn't a familiar smell anywhere—no tea

and ginger from the kitchen, no tatami mats in the living room, no orchids by the window. But it was his father's home. The one place in the whole world his father wanted him to be.

After Kai's mother cried, his father had hugged him, in front of everybody, which Kai had always hated. His father said, "Your uncle Per was the best brother, the best friend, a boy could have. He knows all of the places I love." He loosened his grip on Kai. "When I'm working on all of this"—he waved an arm toward the frantic activity of the power plant—"I want to think of you in those places."

Kai had felt the anxiety of the engineers in the room. His father was looking for an anchor, and Kai could be that for him. Five thousand miles from home, it was all he had to give.

12

"DINNER!" JET HOLLERED out the kitchen door. There was a smear of flour on her forehead and the front of her shirt, a splash of cooking oil on her shorts, and a blob of bread dough in her hair.

Jet waited. There was an answer from her mom but none from Oliver. She looked out the kitchen window at the tree house. It was dumping down rain. Jet sighed and rubbed the last bits of bread dough off her fingers. The pot of chowder was bubbling on the back of the stove. She'd already given the salad a toss. Setting the table was Oliver's job. Where was the twerp? There was no point in yelling. If he was reading he wouldn't hear a tornado. She finally found him in the laundry room, sitting on a pile of towels, under the spell of Sherlock Holmes.

On the way back to the kitchen, Jet hadn't meant to eavesdrop—neither of them had—but they heard Mom say, "Now about Oliver—" just as they passed the living room door. They both stopped in their tracks.

"—and the news," Mom said. "Maybe this isn't how your parents would do this, Kai, but for now, I want us to look at the news after Oliver's asleep. He's a born worrier, and he's only eight. All those terrible pictures and the endless guessing about the things that could still go horribly wrong. . . . It's not good for him."

Oliver turned to Jet. He was the picture of silent outrage. Of all the names to be called—*worrier*. He was working himself up to a shriek of protest. Jet took him by both shoulders and steered him into the kitchen.

Oliver was still sputtering when Jet closed the kitchen door. She handed him a stack of plates.

"Oh, buck up!" Jet said. She grabbed the bowls and followed him to the dining room. "She could have called you a nose picker." They set places around the table. "Or a bed wetter."

Oliver glared. She handed him the basket of silverware.

"Or a banana-slug handler." Jet went on getting

glasses out of the cabinet. "Let's see, what else would be worse? Landlubber? Dredgeling?"

Oliver let out a snort against his will.

"Bet you can think of something better than that."

"Um, detested parasite?" Oliver said thoughtfully. He laid out spoons and forks. "Vile bunch-backed toad!"

He was into it now. He took a few thrusts and swipes with a butter knife.

"Lump of foul deformity! Moldy rogue! Swollen parcel of droppings!"

Everyone agreed reading Shakespeare out loud to Oliver had been a huge mistake.

"That's the spirit," Jet said.

Back in the kitchen, Mom handed Kai a basket with warm bread wrapped in a napkin.

"Per was going to get you a phone on the way home from work today," she said. "But this weather . . ." She gestured at the kitchen window, which was rattling in the wind. "He's in for a rough crossing tonight. We'll get your phone tomorrow."

Jet grabbed the bowl of salad and led Kai to the dining room. Mom followed with the pot of chowder. Kai took a spot beside Oliver, who had shut up the

second his cousin stepped through the door and was now doing a convincing impression of a barnacle.

Jet stifled the impulse to roll her eyes. Mom was going to talk too much, and Oliver wasn't going to talk at all. And Dad was going to be late, maybe hours late. She hadn't had a minute to check the storm tracker on the NOAA website since she started cooking. She was itching to dig out her phone and take a quick look, but Mom had rules about phones and dinner. Commandments, really.

They passed around plates, and Mom launched into the news about the summer festival that was coming up. Kai stared at Jet in a way people didn't usually stare. Jet was not the pretty one, like Skye. For sure she wasn't the curvy one, like Bridgie. At the last sleepover, Bridgie told Jet she'd be super cute if she did a thing with her hair, something about bangs and a swoop. Jet convinced her to give Skye a makeover instead. The two of them had talked about boys nonstop. Bridgie had found something to like about almost everybody, but Skye liked Roland, of all people—some nonsense about black hair and brown eyes. As if good looks made up for bullying people.

So far Jet had only seen her cousin fall asleep, and

already she would bet cash money he had a better personality than Roland. They did have the same color hair and eyes, though. She gave him a closer look. Kai was her only cousin. He didn't look like her—not the nose, not the chin—but they both had freckles. For two awful weeks last October, Roland had called her Spot, and Jet had silently planned his epic downfall.

Mom was still carrying on about the Scandinavian Festival in July. Every now and then Jet tossed the ball to Kai.

"Did you sleep okay?"

Nod. Mumble.

"Play any sports?"

Mumble. Nod.

The wind whistled around the corners of the house, and when the lights flickered Mom lit the candles on the table and in the window, even though the power stayed on. Oliver paddled his spoon around in his soup and cast frequent looks at Dad's empty chair.

"Oliver," Mom said quietly, "if he missed his jump, we'd have heard by now."

"It's been hours," Oliver said. "There aren't supposed to be storms in June."

"Sorry about this, Kai," Mom said. "Per really

wanted to be here for your first dinner, but sometimes crossing the bar takes longer in heavy weather."

Kai looked confused, and Jet wondered if he knew what bar pilots did. Uncle Lars must have told him something, but maybe he focused on the fair-weather crossings. When Dad talked about Uncle Lars being a nuclear engineer, he for sure didn't mention meltdowns. Oliver looked like he was going to be sick. He was a worrier. When he was littler he used to hide under the stairs during stormy crossings. What he really needed was some distraction to get him through.

"It's not the worst storm we've had this year—" Mom began.

"Twenty-foot swells and thirty-knot winds. Tricky!" Jet barged in. She glanced at Oliver to see if he'd make a connection to the Beaufort wind scale. If she could get him thinking about science, he'd stop thinking about Dad.

"He's piloted in far worse," Mom said. "I'm sure he'll be just—"

"It's the Graveyard of the Pacific!" Jet said, changing tactics. She turned to Kai. "Most dangerous dozen nautical miles in the hemisphere. Dozens of shipwrecks happen here. Hundreds!"

Oliver was a big fan of local history. He could lead tours, easy.

"The *Peacock*," Oliver said very quietly.

"Eighteen forty-one," Jet announced with a flourish.

"The *Grand Republic*. No, the *Great Republic*."

"Eighteen seventy-nine."

"The *Peter Iredale*."

They ping-ponged names of wrecked ships and dates back and forth for ten minutes.

"But . . . ," Jet said with a smile.

"But Daddy's never lost a ship," Oliver said.

"Not even one pound of cargo," Jet added proudly.

"So no need to worry," Mom said. Oliver started eating, and she breathed a sigh of relief.

"Good!" Jet said, completely satisfied with herself. "So."

She turned to Kai, who suddenly looked like he'd lost his last friend. Maybe shipwrecks were the wrong topic for a boy who'd narrowly escaped drowning. Jet had a gift for saying exactly the wrong thing. She had a feeling this was one of her especially gifted moments. Even her mother seemed at a loss for words. Jet searched for a not-ocean topic of conversation. School? Nope, his had been swallowed by the tsunami. Music?

Movies? They would be on his phone. Also lost forever. Better to get him thinking about something else.

"Mom, can we take Kai to Fort Clatsop tomorrow?"

"Great idea!" Mom immediately snapped up the new topic of conversation and launched into the story of Lewis and Clark.

Finally Dad's truck rolled up the driveway. Mom set down her fork and closed her eyes for a moment. Jet felt a stab of guilt. Mom worried, too. If Jet became a pilot, Mom would worry even more. She'd seen her mom pace the front porch in a storm. She knew what the candle in the window meant.

13

KAI HEARD A truck in the driveway and saw Aunt Karin breathe a sigh of relief. Jet brought the candle from the window back to the table.

"Dad!" Oliver yelled. He raced to the back door. There was a thud and a grunt from the kitchen.

"Aargh! Woman of the house! Save me from this troll!" Gales of laughter came through the door. "I've met my death, woman! I'll never move again."

"Whatever will you do?" Aunt Karin said calmly, in spite of the splat of heavy wet things dropping on the floor.

Oliver begged for news about the storm. It took only a little bit of begging.

"It was a fearsome thing! Waves as big as sky-scrapers! Wind roaring like a jet engine!"

"Were there pirates?"

"It wasn't a fit day for pirates of any stripe. Not even Vikings would have dared a crossing."

"Aw, no pirates?"

"But there were dragons!"

"Ooh!"

"Two of them!"

"No!"

"Yes! Never a more deadly pair. They were last seen swallowing a cruise ship whole."

"You had better not be giving my child nightmares," Aunt Karin said, a little louder.

Captain Ellstrom came to the kitchen door, filling it completely.

Kai stared. The man was as tall as his father, with the same blond hair and blue eyes. They could have been twins, except that where his father had the pale and clean-shaven face of a scientist, his uncle was as red-faced and wrinkled as a rice farmer. His cousin had both arms clamped firmly around Uncle Per's neck and dangled down his back. Uncle Per stopped at Kai's seat and reached out to shake his hand.

"They were *ryūjin,* I'm sure of it," he went on. "Did I say it right?"

Kai nodded, feeling a little shell-shocked.

"Ryūjin!" Uncle Per continued in the same booming voice as before. "Cruise-ship-swallowing dragons, brought over by some foreign visitor, no doubt." He winked at Kai.

"The dragons would have gotten clean away, but they had to stop and spit out all the Finns and Norwegians aboard."

Oliver giggled.

"You're not with the Sons of Norway, are you?" Uncle Per said to Kai. "The Finnish Brotherhood?"

"I don't think so!" Jet said with obvious scorn.

"God help us! He's one of those black-haired Irish, like your pirate brother!" He turned and glared at Aunt Karin. One sharp look from her, and Uncle Per burst out laughing.

"Your nephew is as Swedish as your own children," Aunt Karin said.

Kai looked from one face to the next. Who shouts in his own house? Makes fun of a guest? What was the matter with these people?

"Does he wash dishes?" Uncle Per said, still much louder than necessary.

"I'm sure he'll learn," Aunt Karin said.

"Heave him overboard the minute he gives you trouble."

"Per." Karin folded her arms and gave him another look. He grinned broadly, strode up to her chair with Oliver still dangling off the back of him, and gave her a kiss.

"Last windstorm of the season," he said quietly. "I promise."

She sighed. "There never used to be storms like this in June." She stroked his still-damp hair.

"I could retire," he said softly. "We could move somewhere where there isn't weather of any kind." He kissed her again. "The moon, for example."

Kai looked from his aunt to his uncle. He had never heard his parents talk to each other like this. For sure he'd never seen them kissing.

Per mistook Kai's look of surprise. "*P-E-R* is the correct spelling for Peter."

"It's the Swedish spelling for Peter," Jet said. "You'll get used to it. At least you're not—"

"Danish!" Per laughed. "Or worse yet, German!"

"Or a river pilot," Jet finished with a wicked smile. "That would just be embarrassing."

"Enough," Karin said, and gave Per a nudge toward his chair.

"All right then," Per said. He turned and then jumped with exaggerated surprise at the empty chair.

"Where's my Oliver?" He turned from side to side. Oliver held on tighter and stifled a laugh.

"You didn't lose your brother again, did you?" He glared at Jet.

"Dad," Jet rolled her eyes.

Oliver burst out laughing.

"Wait! I can hear him. Oliver! Where are you, boy?" He took a lap around the table in a few long strides with Oliver giggling even more loudly. He stopped and gave the breadbasket a meaningful look. He lifted up the napkin that covered the bread, peeked underneath, and then heaved a sigh of relief.

"Oh, Per, for heaven's sake!"

"He's . . . um . . . behind you," Kai said.

"Behind me?" He reached back and grabbed Oliver around the middle, lifted him up over his head, and held him upside down. "Well, what do you have to say for yourself?"

Oliver reached his hands for the floor as if he were

trying to swim out of his dad's grasp. "Put me down. Please?"

"Eh? What was that?"

Oliver took a breath and let out the biggest dinosaur roar he could muster.

"My ferocious," Uncle Per said proudly as he set the still-wiggling Oliver down headfirst in his chair.

"The boy who kicks over a dish at this table will live to regret it!" Aunt Karin said.

Both Oliver and his dad froze. Uncle Per silently turned Oliver right-side up, dusted him off, and arranged him so he was sitting up straight with shoulders back and hands in his lap. He turned to his wife, gestured in Oliver's direction with a flourish, and gave her a smile that begged for approval.

Aunt Karin was laughing quietly through the whole charade. "Yes, thank you. That'll do."

Jet leaned across the table. "Sorry," she said to Kai. "He's like this. You'll get used to it."

Uncle Per turned to Kai. "*Yoku kitana.* Welcome aboard, Kai," he said quietly. "Our home is yours. Stay forever if you like." He put a hand on Kai's shoulder. "Or for as long as you can stand our ill-mannered company."

Kai had no idea how to respond. His uncle looked so familiar—the way he smiled more on one side of his mouth than the other, the deepness of his voice. But he seemed twice as big and half as smart as his own father. Kai opened his mouth, but nothing came out.

"You do belong here, Kai," Uncle Per said. "Seafaring men in our family have lived in this house for a hundred and thirty-seven years."

Kai glanced around the room. Not a single thing felt familiar.

"And stouthearted women," Uncle Per added, a little more loudly. He turned to Jet. She stiffened in her chair.

"What have you been up to?"

"Stuff," Jet said.

Oliver said something about the park with a mouth full of bread and chowder.

"Good weather for a sail."

There was a long pause.

Is she in trouble? Kai wondered. For sailing? His father had often spoken of sailing with Uncle Per when they were boys. He'd loved to sail and was happy when Ojī-san took Kai out in the *Ushio-maru*. Wouldn't Uncle Per want his daughter to love the sea as much

as he did? Kai took in the way Jet was sitting, hands jammed in pockets, chin up, mouth in a resolute line.

Aunt Karin was looking, too. "Whatever this is about, you'll settle it away from my table."

Jet dropped her eyes to her plate, and Uncle Per smiled at her tenderly. "Talk when you're ready," he said.

Jet nodded without looking up.

"And until you're ready, stay off the water. Do you hear me?"

"Yes."

Her voice was different in that *yes,* and Oliver hopped up without a word, ran around the table, and leaned his head on Jet's shoulder like he was her pet puppy. She messed up his hair and then kissed the top of his head.

"Go away," she said, back to her normal voice.

Oliver clamped his arms around her and squeezed.

"I mean it, Oliver. If you don't eat more than that, you're going to shrink." She waved in the direction of his half-finished soup bowl. "Go on," Jet said more gently, giving him a shove.

"Dad, how did you say hello today?" Oliver asked. He broke up pieces of bread in his soup.

"I said *'namaste'* to my old friend Captain Gupta from . . ."

"Mumbai," Jet said.

"And what do you think he was carrying?" Uncle Per went on.

"Computer parts? Clothes?" Oliver said.

They went on guessing ships, first the country and then the cargo, as relaxed in their talking as they'd been stilted before.

"Story after dishes!" Uncle Per announced when they were done eating. Oliver hopped off his chair and started bussing the table at warp speed.

"Make yourself useful," Uncle Per said to Kai. "If you can't find something you need, ask."

"Let him be," Aunt Karin said. "He's had a very long day."

"I don't mind," Kai said. He stood up. "Please. It would be familiar."

"All right then." Aunt Karin smiled. "Don't let Jet boss you around in there."

Kai followed his cousins into the kitchen. Jet swept the floor. There was a teetering stack of dishes to the left of the sink and not a trace of a dishwasher any-where. Oliver set the last of the plates beside the sink

and dashed off to the living room with a thick book under his arm. Kai ran the hot water and looked under the sink for soap and a sponge. Jet stood by with a dish towel to dry and put away.

He and his *obā-san* had done this together a thousand times. He told her the news from school. She told him ghost stories. The rhythm of it was familiar, and he didn't have to think about whether he was doing it right. A clean dish is a clean dish, no matter where in the world you've landed.

14

It took three days, but Kai finally got his parents on the phone. The sound of a voice in Japanese, the music of it, almost made him cry. His mother told him to be helpful and kind to his cousins. His father told him he'd get over the jet lag eventually. They both sounded dead tired. Neither of them mentioned his grandparents, and he couldn't bring himself to ask. Kai felt better after talking to them, but he felt worse, too. He should be doing something to help—anything.

"Want to go to town?" Jet said as they sat on the porch with their breakfast cereal. "Mom said we could. It's kind of boring, except for the pool and the movies. My favorite is the maritime museum."

"Okay! Sure!" Kai said, wincing at both the

interruption and the fake enthusiasm. "I mean . . . if you want to."

"Of course." Jet smiled. "Or there's bowling, if you're really into that, and um . . ."

"Isn't there anything I could do around here to help?" Kai said.

"Help?" Jet looked confused.

"Maybe I could bike to the fish market for your mom?" There must be a fish market. He went every afternoon for his grandma.

"Or work on the garden?" Kai didn't want to go so far as to point, but there were weeds all over the place.

"Oh," Jet looked around the yard, crestfallen. "Yeah, I should totally mow the grass."

At last! Something useful!

"Plenty of time for that later," Jet charged on. "There's a bookstore and a comic shop. What do you think? Oh, and there's a skate park. Are you a skater?"

Kai gave up. There was no helping this girl.

Jet had been his faithful tour guide for three days. She had tried so hard to be nice, but the very fact that she was trying made Kai long to say, "Please just shut up!" It wasn't her fault, but he was weary of her, and the thought of spending the rest of the summer

together made him want to run away and live in a cave. Oliver, who hadn't said a word to him, was well on his way to being cousin of the year.

But he'd promised his mother he'd be kind to his cousins. And his father had been thrilled to hear him talk about Fort Clatsop and the Goonies House and all the famous spots in Astoria. He'd told Kai again the story of winning the Treasure Island Race with Uncle Per. Kai forced a smile.

"The comic shop sounds good."

Kai had—used to have—an entire shelf in his bedroom for his favorite manga.

"Or the museum is fine, too," he added. If he couldn't help out, at least he could be agreeable. "Do you like that one better?"

"It's my favorite," Jet said.

Kai let Jet take the lead. They fixed up Uncle Per's old ten-speed bike, grabbed helmets, and headed down the hill. They passed a school and then a skate park that was packed with kids their age. Kai was sure they were going to stop and say hello, but Jet rocketed past them with barely a glance.

Once they were on level ground by the river, Kai looked toward the ocean. Good. So that would be east.

He looked in the other direction. The sun was still rising on the upstream end of the river.

The ocean was on the wrong side of the land.

Kai couldn't get used to it; he felt lost everywhere he went.

He followed Jet along the boardwalk. Astoria was bigger than Ikata, but so much felt heartbreakingly like home. The familiar smell of machine oil and fish haunted the cannery, where boats brought their catch to be weighed and sorted. A cluster of sailboats zigzagged through the chop on the Washington side of the river. Jet stopped at a gray-shingled building with a curving roof that said COLUMBIA RIVER MARITIME MUSEUM on the front.

While Jet was busy locking up their bikes, Kai edged closer to the river, feeling his heart race as he did.

He looked for the nearest street that led away from the water. It was steep. Good.

He checked the waterline. He fixed his gaze on the sailboats and forced himself to breathe steadily.

He checked the waterline again. Was it the same? Of course it was the same. The ground was holding still.

Was it? He looked at the tops of the power lines. They weren't swaying. Everything was fine.

Kai leaned against the light buoy that was on display in front of the museum. He rested his head against the cold steel. Jet lag was not his problem. The panic was going to kill him.

He looked at the sailboats again. He missed the feeling of a boat rocking to one side as it caught the wind, the pressure of water against the tiller, the rattle of the sail. His grandfather had been a fisherman. He and Kai would hang out with the old-timers at the marine supply store. Sometimes a younger fisherman would ask them to help fix a boat. And if the day was especially fine for sailing, they'd take out the *Ushio-maru* and sail along the peninsula to look for dolphins or drop a fishing line, or just to admire the beauty of the mountains and the quiet of open water. Kai knew his father and uncle had sailed together as children in a boat called the *Saga*. He'd been hoping to see it, but nobody had mentioned it, and he couldn't quite bring himself to ask.

Kai turned away from the water. The *Ushio-maru* was gone, along with everything else. No amount of dreaming would bring it back.

15

JET WAS RELIEVED to see Kai walk away. He'd been right under her nose for what felt like every minute of the last three days. And to make matters worse, he was relentlessly polite the entire time. He was patient with Oliver's shyness. He did chores without stalling or complaining. Jet spun her bike lock and yanked it open. It was going to be a long summer.

At least Kai hadn't asked to go skateboarding. The whole gang from school was there, and Roland was in the thick of it, showing off skateboard tricks while Skye and Bridgie just sat around and admired him.

She wasn't being fair, and she knew it. Kai had lost everything. The reactor where his parents worked was still in danger, and his grandparents were still missing. A sensible person, a kind person, would just forget about her own problems and help her cousin cheer up. A polite person would be, well, more like Kai, who had apparently never had an unkind thought in his life.

Unlike Jet, who had imagined sinking the *Viking* and its obnoxious red sail approximately twenty times a day. It was bad enough that Roland stole her friend. Did he have to steal her racing partner, too?

To make matters worse, she'd been too busy to fix the *Saga*. She knew she should just tell her dad. Jet kicked her bike tire. No talk with Dad, no sailing. Fine. It shouldn't be so hard. It's not like her dad was widely known for saintly behavior. But the thought of telling him her mistake, of saying it out loud. When she'd been so stupid! She couldn't swallow it.

Captain Dempsey would never have done this. She wasn't the first woman bar pilot ever because she had a legacy of fathers and uncles who were also bar pilots. She was a master mariner, and she was perfect— invitation-to-the-White-House perfect. The sea stories she told got written up in magazines. For sure she didn't forget to check the tide. If Jet was going to be the second woman bar pilot in history, she was going to have to be better than perfect.

Jet turned her attention to the gigantic window at

the front of the museum. It showed her favorite exhibit, the most dramatic one in the whole museum, a full-size coast guard lifeboat in mid-rescue on heavy seas. The lifeboat was standing on its stern, riding up a thirty-foot wave made of plaster. The guardsmen mannequins were all in full foul-weather gear: helmets, red jackets, safety vests, and lifelines clipped to the rails. One of them was tossing a life ring to a drowning man. The scene towered over the sidewalk. Inside the museum they piped in the sound of wind and crashing waves and the growl of a lifeboat motor. It was awesome.

Dad knew plenty of Coasties. Jet loved it when he invited them home for dinner. They were big and loud and full of wild stories about rescues made in eighty-knot winds and forty-foot seas. Jet looked at the familiar display, thinking about the tsunami that just came through. It was nothing like the usual storms. The sky was clear, wind calm, visibility perfect. There wasn't the up and down of storm swells. The water rose relentlessly in one push. They'd had plenty of warning to get to high ground. By the time the tsunami came ashore, there wasn't anybody left to rescue.

What did the coast guard do in Japan? she wondered. They wouldn't have had any time to clear their

harbors. Jet got a twinge in her stomach. There hadn't been one lone fisherman in the water needing rescue. There had been hundreds.

She stepped back from the window, nausea setting in. This was a terrible idea. Kai didn't want to see this. Her heart started to race. I have to get him out of here, she thought. Jet spun around and nearly knocked Kai over. He was standing directly behind her, dead silent, his eyes locked on the drowning man.

16

"WAIT. KAI, DON'T look," Jet said. She pulled him away. "I'm sorry. Let's just go."

Kai took a step back, eyes still locked on the rescue display.

"I'm sorry," Jet said. "I don't know what I was thinking."

Kai shook himself and looked away. If only there had been a rescue boat like this one, with life jackets and lifelines. If he'd run faster and gotten to his grandparents sooner. If they'd gone into the hills instead of to the fish cannery.

"It must be a good feeling," he said quietly. "To rescue people."

"Yeah." Jet continued to edge away. "The Coasties

we know are really great. Most of them are a little on the loud and crazy side."

She took a few steps farther.

"Like my dad."

Kai opened his mouth to say something. Jet had a way of telling the truth even when it was not the polite thing to say.

"No. Seriously," she went on. "Everybody thinks Dad is a little bit crazy. Big Per, everybody's got a story about him." Kai followed her away from the river. "How about your dad?" she asked. "Are there funny stories?"

"Not really. Sometimes when there's a festival, and it's late at night, my father tells the story about how his nickname used to be Little Lars. That usually gets a laugh."

"Bet it wasn't easy being my dad's baby brother," Jet said. "Well, as soon as your dad fixes up the reactor, he'll be a big hero. Dad is always bragging on how crazy smart Uncle Lars is. Nuclear submarines is the brainiest job in the whole navy."

Kai turned away from his cousin. He hated blushing. It was the worst part of being paler than his

classmates. "He's got a good team," Kai said firmly. "If there's a solution, they'll find it together."

"Do you know what my dad says about Uncle Lars?"

Kai shook his head.

"He says, 'It's not just that my brother is smart. Lars is a lot braver than me. Braver by a mile—a nautical mile.' Do you know why he says that?"

"Because a nautical mile is longer than a land mile," Kai said, smiling.

"Longer by 1.1—" Jet began.

"5078 U.S. customary miles," Kai finished.

How about that, Kai thought. An inch of common ground.

EVENTUALLY THEY CAME to the comic shop. The display window had a life-size Spider-Man doll scaling the glass. Darth Vader lurked in a corner. Flyers for Rose City Comic Con were taped to the window. Inside, Kai flipped through the bins of manga until he found his favorite from when he was eight years old. Oliver had barely spoken three words to him in the last three days, but he loved to read. Kai was hoping Oliver would love good old Naruto as much as he had. But maybe not. Would Oliver really admire a manga

hero? They didn't indulge in the single-handed crashing about that heroes did in American movies.

Maybe Kai was the one who should change. Maybe
Captain America was the key to understanding his
American cousins. He grabbed three comics from the
Captain America bin, found himself a spot on the floor,
and began studying.

A little while later Jet came and sat beside him.

"Hungry? There's a teriyaki place on the corner,"
she said.

Kai had been smelling the teriyaki and getting
more homesick by the minute.

"McDonald's would be great. You have to drive for
hours to get there from my town. Is there one nearby?"

"Right this way," Jet said.

Kai bought one Captain America for Oliver and one
Naruto, just in case. Jet waved good-bye to the shop
girl and headed them down Commercial Street.

"Best to get McDonald's when it's just the two of
us," Jet said. "Mom's kind of into the healthy food.
It will get better when Dad's shift is over, and he has
twenty days in a row off the river. Then Mom will be
drawing her comic book night and day, and Dad will
do all the shopping and cooking. It'll be barbecue

chicken and the good kind of cookies for dinner all the time."

"Uncle Per cooks?"

"With gusto!" Jet said. "It's a little bit frightening. So what's your favorite at McDonald's?"

"Shrimp burger and potato pie."

"Potato pie? They have potato pie at McDonald's?"

"With bacon. What else would you eat with a shrimp burger?"

Jet stopped walking. "Potato pie. Really? I thought the menu was the same everywhere."

"Huh," Kai said. "Me too."

The big differences in America—like everybody speaking English and all the money being green, Kai had expected. But the other stuff, the menu at McDonald's, the gigantic grocery stores, the way people hugged each other for no reason—those differences made him feel like he'd landed on the surface of the moon.

"Do you want to go somewhere else?" Jet asked.

His father had mentioned something on the phone about the best soda shop in the universe. Kai couldn't remember the name.

"Is there a place to get milk shakes?"

Jet did an about-face. "Custard King to the rescue!"

she announced. "Let's get three milk shakes and call it lunch."

Ten minutes later they were perched on a brick wall, watching river traffic go by and rotating sips between three milk shakes.

"Perfect day for a sail," Kai said, nodding toward the sailboats that darted back and forth between fishing boats on the Columbia.

Jet sighed. "Yes, perfect," she said.

"My dad told me stories about a boat he and Uncle Per sailed in the Astoria Regatta when they were boys. Do you still have it?"

Jet nodded, took the last slurp of the chocolate-hazelnut shake, and pitched the empty cup into the trash at the edge of the parking lot.

"I kind of made a mistake," she said. She pulled her knees up to her chest and rested her chin on them. "I broke it."

"Broke it?"

"A little bit. I didn't actually sink it. Not completely. I kind of ran into something. Long story."

"But we can fix it, right?" Kai wiggled the straw around in the strawberry shake to get the last bit.

"I don't know," Jet said. "I've never done this before."

"Can I take a look?"

"You know how to patch a boat?" Jet perked up.

Kai nodded. He couldn't quite bring himself to talk about fixing boats with his *ojī-san,* so instead he said, "My mom had a sailboat called the *Ushio-maru.*"

"Cool name," Jet said. "Does it mean something?"

"It means *tide,* or it can mean *opportunity.*"

Kai could picture every line of his boat, the curve of her sails against the blue of the sky and the deeper blue of the Uwa Sea, the red-and-white rigging ropes, the polished mahogany of the trim pieces.

"When my father was on one of his submarine cruises, and they had liberty in Japan, he saw my mother sailing, and they got to talking about her boat because it was like the one he had when he was a boy. That's how they met."

When he'd left Ikata, Kai looked for his boat in the water and among the ruins on the shore. The marina was still under drifts of mud and great tangles of broken steel and piles of shattered timbers. He'd only looked for one second, but that second of looking played over and over in his head.

"Hello," Jet said a few moments later in a singsong

voice. "Earth to Kai!" She tilted her head to the side to look at him. "Will you show me how to fix my boat?"

Kai swam up out of his memories. "Sure," he said.

Fixing one sailboat wasn't much, but in a universe of broken things, he was grateful for something to mend.

17

JET AND KAI collected their bikes and rode up the boardwalk to the marine hardware store. Jet described the size and shape of the holes in the *Saga*, and Kai filled up a basket with what they needed: cloth and resin, but also acetone, brushes and rags, a box cutter, and turpentine for cleaning up.

When they got to the sailing club, Captain Chandler's van was parked in the drive, and the red sailboat was at the dock. Great, Jet thought. Roland. Just who I don't want to deal with right now. But Roland was nowhere in sight. It was only Beck and his dad.

When Jet opened the shed door, Kai actually gasped at the sight of the *Saga* and ran his hand lovingly over the bow.

"Is it really the same boat our fathers won the Treasure Island Race in?" Kai said.

"Yup," Jet said. "They were fourteen and thirteen when they won, back in the age of dinosaurs."

"He has stories about this boat," Kai said. "A lot of stories."

Jet smiled as she watched her cousin look at the *Saga* with his hands as much as with his eyes. It was the first moment she'd seen him look relaxed since he arrived. He was finally on familiar ground.

"Okay, what was that first step?" she said.

Kai launched into a description of the process. He'd been more chatty in the last hour than he'd been for three days. This was what she missed about hanging out with Beck. He liked to build stuff. Last summer they'd worked for weeks on the tree house and its rock wall and zip line. Over at Beck's house they'd built a rope bridge and an archery range. Their dads had helped, especially Captain Chandler, but most of it was just her and Beck and a box of tools and one delicious building problem after another.

She stole a look at the red sailboat. Roland still hadn't shown up. Near as she could tell from

eavesdropping on the boys' table at lunch, all Beck and Roland ever did was play video games. Jet had been hoping all school year long that Beck would get bored of it and come over to build stuff again in the summer, but maybe getting Roland to sail with him was Beck's answer to that problem.

Captain Chandler had his wheelchair alongside the catamaran and was helping Beck with the rigging. It tugged at Jet's heart to see Captain Chandler on the edge of what he loved and was no longer able to do. Jet turned her attention back to the *Saga*. She prepped the site of the hole while Kai cut a patch of fiberglass to size. The resin had a sharp metallic smell. She held the patch in place while Kai painted the resin on. He was easy to work with—careful to get things right but cheerful, too. He laughed at himself when he forgot and used the Japanese word for *brush* or *rag*.

They were starting on the second patch when Beck walked up.

"Hey, guys," he said, a little shyly.

"Hey," Jet answered. She was glad to see him but wary. Roland never missed a chance to put her down, and Beck never took sides. It was hard to know where she stood with him.

"So you'll be able to fix her then?" Beck asked.

"Yup," Jet said, still cautious.

Beck leaned in for a closer look at the patch. "Are you going to race?"

"Um, well . . . Beck, this is my cousin, Kai," she said, to stall his question about the race. "He's visiting from Japan."

"Beautiful boat," Kai said, nodding in the direction of the catamaran.

"Do you sail?"

"Yeah," Kai said. "I had a wooden boat a lot like this one."

"Is it gone?" Beck asked. "In the . . . er . . . I mean . . ."

Jet winced. She'd tried so hard not to make a thing of Kai's troubles.

"It's gone," Kai said.

There was an awkward pause.

"I hear those Hobies can be tricky to handle," Jet said.

"We nearly dumped it over twice on our first try," Beck said.

Good! Jet thought. She resisted saying it aloud.

"We're getting the hang of it, though," Beck added.

I should say something nice, Jet thought. Nothing but wisecracks came to mind. It was almost like she was turning into the girl version of Roland. There was another awkward pause.

Beck looked down at his shoes. "I need your help, actually."

"What's up?" Jet said.

"It's my dad. He's a little bit—"

"Oh my gosh! Is he okay?" Jet said, imagining the worst. She turned to Kai. "Captain Chandler is a bar pilot, like Dad, but he got hurt last year, and now he can't walk. But he will. He's going to get new legs." She spun to face Beck. "Right?"

"September," Beck said.

"September? That's forever!"

"I know," Beck said. "And it's killing him to wait. He keeps thinking he can do stuff. It's driving my mom crazy, he keeps . . ."

"Falling?" Jet asked.

"This time he's just stuck."

Jet stood on tiptoes to look over at the red sailboat. Captain Chandler was lying on the trampoline deck.

"He really misses being on the water," Beck said.

"He got the catamaran because he thought the different kind of deck would make it easier for him to move around."

"How exactly is he stuck?" Kai asked.

"Come look," Beck said.

They walked over to the dock. Captain Chandler was lying on his back in a T-shirt and shorts. The ends of his amputated legs were covered with what looked like cream-colored knit hats. He had a cap pulled low over his eyes.

"Hi, Jet," he called out as they came near. He turned to Kai. "Hey, you're Lars's boy! Per said you were over for the summer. I met your dad years ago."

Kai nodded, stopping just short of the bow he usually gave his friends' parents.

"Don't you fret about the news, now. There is a solution to that reactor problem, and Lars is the man to find it."

"He has a good team," Kai said.

"The best, I'm sure," Captain Chandler said. "Problems aplenty right here, though." The trampoline deck sagged under his weight, making a hole he couldn't climb out of. "I think what we need is a rocket pack,"

he said with a wink. "Where's Iron Man when you need him?"

"How about a construction crane?" Jet suggested. "Or maybe a catapult?"

"Artillery usually is the answer," Captain Chandler said with a laugh. "Beck, get the national guard on the phone. We'll blast our way out of this!"

"Dad!" Beck sighed. "Can't we just—" He pulled out his phone.

"No need to trouble your mom," Captain Chandler said quickly.

"Actually what we need is a big piece of cloth," Kai said. Everybody turned to look at him. "You can roll, right?" he asked Captain Chandler.

"Sure."

"So if we slide a sheet under you, then we can tug you to the side, where you can reach your chair."

"I remember that," Captain Chandler said. "A nurse did it while I was in the hospital. She was a bitty thing, but she moved me, no problem."

"Let's get the jib sail from the *Saga*," Jet said. "It's big enough."

"Okay," Beck said. "But how are we going to get him back in the chair?"

"That's a problem." Kai looked around. "We need him to be up higher than the chair."

"If the boat was on the trailer, he would be," Beck said.

"So we just need to get someone to drive the trailer down the boat ramp," Jet said.

"No problem." Captain Chandler fished in his pocket and tossed a set of keys to Beck.

"He lets you drive?" Kai and Jet said together, him with admiration and her with alarm.

"Only in reverse." Beck flashed a broad smile.

He got in the driver's seat and gunned the engine. Kai waved Beck down the boat ramp. It took him three tries to get the trailer lined up straight. Jet attached the bow rope to the windlass and cranked the handle to pull the boat onto the trailer. Once the boat was secure, Kai took over, showing Beck and Jet how the sliding-sheet trick worked. Beck wheeled the chair into place. Even with their best efforts, Captain Chandler fell the last foot or so into the chair.

"No blood, no foul!" he announced once the wincing subsided. "Let's just keep this adventure to ourselves, shall we?" He gave his son a meaningful nod.

"Who's telling?" Beck said, holding up both hands. "Do I ever tell Mom?"

"So, my hearties," Captain Chandler said, looking from Jet to Kai. "Will you take your reward in ice cream?"

"Gosh," Jet said. "Love to, but we had ice cream for lunch."

"How about a sail?" Beck said.

Jet had been telling herself all through the rescue operation that the *Viking* wasn't such a pretty boat, and it wasn't one bit faster than her faithful old *Saga*. Lies. Jet's shoulders slumped. She'd love to give the catamaran a try. But she should finish fixing her own boat. And she was grounded from the water. Technically her dad hadn't said she couldn't sail in someone else's boat, but she was not going to push her luck.

"I'm sorry, Beck. I'm sort of grounded."

"Oh." Beck shrugged and started walking toward the van.

"Wait! Want to come over tomorrow and build something?"

"No thanks," Beck said. "Roland and the guys are having a gaming thing. It goes all day." He opened the

side doors of the van and pushed the button for the wheelchair lift.

"Some other time then," Jet said.

"Sure," Beck said.

But Jet's heart sank as they drove away. For a minute there she was close, but now she wondered if they'd ever be friends again.

18

JET'S ALARM WENT off the next morning. She rolled over and hit the snooze button so hard she knocked the clock to the floor. A beam of light poked through her drapes like an accusing finger. Jet pulled her pillow over her head.

She hadn't talked to her dad last night. She'd had good intentions. She even knew what she wanted to say. And then Dad brought Captain Dempsey and a bunch of the other bar pilots over for dinner, along with a sea captain from his last crossing. They sat out in the yard, feasting on crab and salmon and cucumber salad and home-brewed root beer. They talked up the moon. The mariners had been everywhere, through all the most difficult passages: the

Bosporus, the Panama, the Suez. They had a thousand stories.

Oliver eventually nodded off in a lawn chair, still sticky from the marshmallows they'd roasted. Kai snuck inside to catch up on the news from home. But Jet got caught up in the storytelling as she always did, not even caring that the truth was showing a little wear, only knowing that she wanted sea stories of her own to tell.

Now it was morning, and she still hadn't talked to her dad. Kai had been on the phone since sunup. Her mom had closed the living room door at first light. She'd tied up her hair in a bandana and turned on the Argentine tangos she always listened to when she was drawing a girl superhero. The rule was no disturbing her while she was drawing, but Jet couldn't have disturbed her with the drum line from a marching band. When Mom was working she only stopped for coffee.

"Taking Oliver to swim lessons," Dad trumpeted from the driveway. The van doors slammed, and off they went.

Jet crawled out of bed and got dressed. Kai went to the computer and gobbled up stories and videos

about the tsunami like a starving man. There were Pop-Tarts on the counter and leftover pizza slices in the fridge, clear evidence that Dad was off his piloting rotation and had taken command of the kitchen. Jet snagged a cupcake and headed out to the barn.

What if her dad said no? She could do all the apologizing in the world, and he could decide it wasn't enough to make up for running the *Saga* aground and nearly sailing into a shipping lane. Jet licked the frosting from the top of her cupcake. Forget the race. What if he never let her sail again, ever? What if he wouldn't let her go to the Merchant Marine Academy?

She slid open the barn door. The far end of the barn was stacked with boxes and outgrown bikes. Once upon a time her great-great-grandparents kept a team of horses and a farm wagon. Family legend had it that during the Depression, her great-grandma had raised goats in the barn and kept the entire bar pilots' association from starving with goat cheese and home-grown vegetables. The stalls were gone, but you could see the wear mark on the floor where the stall doors had swung open.

Her father's desk stood against the wall of the barn, beneath his bar pilot's license. It was the last

in a row of seven framed certificates that belonged to grandfathers and uncles clear back to 1875. Per Ellstrom was up there twice, in 1875 and 1999. Grandpa Lars had a license from 1969. There were two Ivars and an Oliver.

Jet had pictured the eighth pilot's license in that row a hundred times—Captain Bridget Jane Ellstrom—written in fancy type with gold curlicues around the edge and the red-and-white pilot's flag at the top. A pilot needed a master mariner's license and a bunch of years as captain of a ship, too. That would take time. But Jet also knew that on the pilot's exam, she'd have to draw the entire nautical chart of the Columbia Bar from memory. She didn't have to wait to start learning that.

She rifled through the drawers of the desk and turned up a few pencils, a pocketknife, and a pad of paper. The NOAA nautical charts were in the filing cabinet. She flipped through them until she found the one marked 18521—the Columbia from the Pacific Ocean to Harrington Point.

She spread it out on the desk and began with mile zero, the spot where the ships' entrance range first met the full force of the river current. The waters off

Clatsop Spit were deadly shallow, and the ship channel swung wide around them, and then narrowed to a space barely wide enough for two ships to pass side by side. Jet faithfully copied each buoy. A dotted line on the chart connected the entrance range with the Cape D lighthouse. Jet pictured herself on the bridge of a ship, guiding it into the river by the same light her great-great-grandfather used a hundred and forty years ago. She copied the names on her chart: Peacock Spit, Sand Island, Jetty Lagoon, Point Adams, the Desdemona Sands. She was so absorbed in her work, she didn't hear the door open.

When Kai said "What are you doing?" she nearly jumped out of her skin.

"Nothing," Jet said automatically.

She flipped over her map and stood up to block his view of the desk. Except for Beck, Jet hadn't talked to anyone about her ambition. For sure she didn't want to talk to her cousin about it. Jet was pretty sure piloting was not a girl job in Japan; it was barely a girl job here.

19

K<small>AI</small> S<small>TOOD</small> B<small>ACK</small> as Jet strode past him to an old chest that stood out a few feet from the wall. Behind it was a metal-and-rope ladder that hung down from the shadows under the roof. She hopped on top of the chest and jumped for the ladder. It struck the barn wall with a thud. Jet scrambled up it, fifteen, maybe twenty feet above the barn floor. Kai could just make out a landing platform at the top no bigger than a fish-house pallet. Jet climbed up and sat, dangling her feet.

Was she hoping he'd go away or daring him to follow? It was hard for Kai to guess. There were plenty of athletic girls at his school. One of them had even run the Tokyo Marathon. But none of the girls were quite so . . . daring? Reckless? No, it wasn't that. She was prickly as a puffer fish. Something was bugging her, and whatever it was, she didn't want to talk about it.

Or maybe she did. Kai was relieved when Aunt Karin finally stopped asking him about his grandparents. But he did want to talk about them, to say what he remembered. He wanted to walk down to the market and talk to Obā-san's best friend at the tea shop. He wanted to help Ojī-san's friends work on their boats. He wanted to make Obā-san's sushi rolls and pick herbs from her garden. It was lonely to live with people who had never known them. Kai gave the ladder a test pull.

"Can I come up?"

"Sure. This platform holds Dad, so for sure it's going to hold both of us," Jet said. She scooted to the edge as Kai made his ascent.

"Well?" she said.

Kai gave the ceiling a look. It was very cobwebby up there.

"So," he said, "this ladder doesn't go anywhere."

"Dad uses it to practice," Jet said. "Ever since Captain Chandler missed the jump, Dad got really serious about daily training."

"The jump?"

"It's how you get from the pilot boat to the ship you're going to guide across the bar. The pilot boat carries you out and pulls up alongside a ship, and the pilot jumps from the deck to the ladder. Then he climbs up as quick as he can, so he doesn't get crushed if a rogue wave bumps the pilot boat up against the ship."

"You're joking!"

"Am not. How do you think Captain Chandler lost his legs?"

"Beck's father?"

Jet nodded. "He was transferring to one of those car carriers in a storm last November. The wind was really strong, and it shifted while he was at the bottom of the ladder."

Jet looked past her dangling sneakers to the barn floor twenty feet below.

"He almost made it," she said quietly. "He was climbing up when the pilot boat bumped into the side of the carrier. His legs were crushed. Lucky he didn't die."

"Isn't there a safer way?"

"Most of the time they use the helicopter and lower the pilot on and off the deck with a cable."

"Uncle Per does this?" Kai said. "He dangles out of

helicopters?" Uncle Per did not seem like the dangling type.

"Nobody's died from the helicopter so far," Jet said. "But they can't use it in fog or snow or freezing rain or winds over fifty knots, so when it's really rough, they take the pilot boat."

"You mean they only jump for the ladder when there's—"

"Heavy seas, blizzards, lightning? Yup."

"Lightning? Whoa!" Kai recalculated his estimation of his uncle's courage.

Jet shrugged. "So good thing Dad practices."

"And you're climbing them because . . ."

"Well . . ."

Jet brushed away a cobweb. She went off on a tangent about spiders. It wasn't like her to hesitate. Well, her parents weren't the most subtle people Kai had ever met. He chose his words pretty carefully around them, too. Aunt Karin was such a talker, and Uncle Per would make a joke out of anything.

"Someone has to be the only woman bar pilot after Captain Dempsey retires," Jet said at last. "Did you know there's only ever been one woman bar pilot?"

Kai shook his head.

"And only two women are pilots on the Columbia. That's just not right! Somebody's got to carry on the tradition. Or what's the point of breaking the barrier in the first place?"

"You really love the ocean, don't you?" Kai said quietly.

"It's so . . . awesome!" Jet said. "How could you not?"

Kai had felt exactly the same for as long as he could remember. He and his dad had already talked about his college plans, his dad arguing for the US Naval Academy and Kai thinking about marine engineering. But now he could barely make himself look at the water. His grandparents' shrine had been washed away. The *ihai* of his great-grandparents was lost. Obā-san had wept for them even as she ran for her life. The funeral tablets would have gone to his mother in time, and eventually they would have been Kai's to protect and honor. But now they were adrift on the ocean, and the mist that hung over the water every morning haunted his dreams.

Even so, Kai missed being on the water. He and his grandfather had a working rhythm when they sailed. Kai loved the physics of how sailing worked, the simple pleasure of catching a fish, and the beauty of his home

waters. Seeing his cousin so ocean crazy made him miss it more.

"You'll be a great pilot," Kai said. "Even my grandfather would say so, and he knows navigation."

Jet smiled. She even blushed a little.

The sound of the van going past the barn and up the driveway reached them. Jet gasped.

"Quick! Down!"

"We aren't supposed to be up here?"

"Not exactly. Go!"

20

KAI GASPED. HE'D never have climbed up if he'd known it was against the rules.

"Hurry!" Jet said through clenched teeth.

"Okay!"

Uncle Per walked down the driveway toward them. The minute Kai was off the ladder, Jet barreled down after him. She ran to the desk, slapped a palm down on a hand-drawn map, and crumpled it into a ball. The door of the barn slid open. Jet stuffed the crumpled map in her pocket and turned away from the desk.

"There you are!" Uncle Per said. "What mischief are you up to in my office?"

"Jet was showing me the . . . ah—"

"Chart of the river!" Jet filled in. She waved at the

chart on the desk. "I was showing him the course for the Treasure Island Race."

"It's true," Kai said, standing shoulder to shoulder with his cousin. "My father has told me so much about the race. I wanted to see for myself."

"You know Uncle Lars would want him to be in it," Jet said. "Be a shame if the *Saga* doesn't sail, even if I don't."

"Giving up, are you?"

"No!" She glared up at her dad.

"Good!" He glared right back.

"Good?"

"Don't you have anything to say to me after all this time?"

Kai's heart was still racing from the climb down the ladder. He could see Jet's hands shaking. She chewed at the corner of her lip.

"Yes," Jet said. She fixed her eyes on the floor and spoke all in a rush.

"I'm sorry, Dad. There's no excuse for what I did. I should have checked the tide. Double-checked. I made a guess, and I was wrong. It was my fault we ran aground. It was my fault that we nearly got swept

into the shipping lane. I never meant to put Oliver in danger. Never!"

Kai took a step back as quietly as he could. For a moment in his mind, he was back in Ikata. When he got to the emergency shelter, he'd hidden in the shadows outside. He knew his principal would shame him for leaving the group, for putting himself above the others, for not falling into line and doing his duty as a proper Japanese boy should. He braced himself for the scolding that would come Jet's way.

"A fair assessment," Uncle Per said. "I appreciate your acceptance of responsibility."

No yelling? Kai looked at his uncle in amazement. The man had a real gift for volume. Even when it was just "pass the salt," you could hear him across the house.

Uncle Per crossed his arms and continued to look sternly at Jet. "And what have you learned?"

"To check the tide?"

There was doubt in her voice. She already knew to check the tide. Uncle Per was waiting for her to say something else.

"You have a phone, yes?" Uncle Per said. "Are you

using it to text all your friends? Listen to pop music? Watch cat videos?"

"You know I'm not like that!"

"So you could use that phone for talking?"

Jet hung her head. Uncle Per put a hand on her shoulder to invite a hug. Jet sighed and leaned in.

Kai let out the breath he didn't realize he'd been holding. His father was like this, too: kind where another man would be stern and calm where another would be angry. Kai had always thought his father was the only one.

"I don't expect you to never make a mistake," Uncle Per said. He kissed the top of her head. "But you have to talk to me, especially when you're in trouble."

"I know," Jet said. "I should have told you way sooner."

"You put your brother in the bad spot of having to tattle on you."

Jet winced.

"So do you think you can find room in your elephant-size pride to apologize to Oliver?"

"Yeah. I'll do it today. Promise."

"Good," Uncle Per said. He glanced over at Kai with a grin. "I didn't apologize to my brother nearly enough.

By my count I owe him nine hundred and seventy-two more."

"That's a lot," Kai said doubtfully.

Uncle Per burst out laughing. "Okay, so I exaggerate a little!" He threw an arm over Kai's shoulder and gave him a hug, just like his own father would. "I hear it's been a little rough out at the reactor," he added, much more gently.

Kai nodded. He'd always cringed at his father's hugs. No one else had a hugging father, but now that he was thousands of miles from home, he missed it.

"Lars'll get the job done. You'll see."

Kai hugged his uncle back. The news on the computer was awful. Each story was worse than the last. His father told him it was going to be okay, but maybe he wasn't telling the truth. Maybe he wasn't allowed to tell the truth.

"Spend a little less time chasing the news and a little more time out in the sun," Uncle Per said. "Knowing you're here, safe and sound, doing all the things he loved when he was a boy, is the medicine that's keeping my brother going. I promise you."

Kai nodded slowly.

"He has a favorite mountain. How about we climb

it together tomorrow and send him a picture from the top?"

Jet edged toward the door to leave them alone.

"I'm not quite done with you, Jet Boat, you future pirate of the high seas!" Uncle Per raised his voice.

"Did I do something else wrong?" Jet said.

"No." Uncle Per smiled. "But I have something for you. An aid to doing things right in the future." He took a thin booklet from his shirt pocket. He thumbed through the first few pages.

"The tide will crest at 7.15 feet at eighteen minutes after noon today." He showed Jet the spot he was reading from on the tide table. "So if I were going to sail on Youngs Bay this morning, any time between eight and noon would be safe. We have nine hours and forty-nine minutes before we lose daylight." He pulled a second tide table out of his pocket and handed it over. "It won't run out of batteries or need the Internet. You can read it in the pouring rain."

Kai turned away so they wouldn't see the tears rising. His *ojī-san* had a paper tide table exactly the same. He kept it in his pocket. He checked it every day. Such a little thing. Why did it choke him up, when all the

hours he'd spent watching video loops of rising water and burning houses didn't? He went over to the desk and pretended to study the chart.

"I check it every morning," Uncle Per went on. "And from now until the day of the race, whether you sail the *Saga* or not, you will tell me the tide and your assessment of when it's safe to sail, taking into consideration all the local conditions. Is that fair?"

"Yeah, but . . . is that all?" Jet looked from the tide table to her dad. "I wrecked the *Saga*!"

"Minor damages."

"Minor?"

"Compared to the loss of life or limb—everything is minor."

Kai thought about Captain Chandler. He'd fallen in the sea somewhere on this very chart of the mouth of the Columbia. The ocean looked easy on paper. Captain Chandler was as tall as Uncle Per and so broad shouldered he made the wheelchair look like a toy. But one rogue wave had crushed him. There was no mercy in the ocean. None.

"What if I hadn't stopped the *Saga*?" Jet said.

"You did stop her," Uncle Per said firmly. "You got

lucky, Jet, and I'm grateful. When you spend your life at sea, luck will always play her part, sometimes running with you and sometimes against."

Kai nodded, lost in his own thoughts.

"I don't love it," Uncle Per went on. "But I've learned to respect that my best effort is not always going to keep me safe. Still, luck favors the well-prepared. Do we have a bargain?"

Jet nodded, and they shook hands. She took a deep breath. Kai looked from one to the other. It was done. She could sail again. Kai traced the shore of Youngs Bay on the chart with his finger. It was only a little smaller than the inlet in front of his home village. His grandfather would have loved to fish there.

"There's still something we have to settle." Uncle Per walked over to the armchair and sat. "You haven't told me the story of it."

"Story?" Jet said, looking from her dad to Kai.

"Waiting!" Uncle Per folded his arms across his chest.

"But . . . it was a disaster," Jet said. "Mistakes from start to finish."

"A sea story is nothing but the run of luck that didn't kill you. Come on now. Out with it!"

Kai pulled up the office chair and gave her an encouraging nod.

Uncle Per leaned forward with anticipation. "Regale us! Embellish! Your cousin there has probably got a million fishing stories. Am I right?"

Kai held up his hands in surrender. People did not just bust out in stories at the drop of a hat. There was the expected back and forth of asking and saying no. But his grandpa did have sea stories. Ojī-san was a great teller.

"You're not going to let your cousin have a better story than you, are you?" Uncle Per said with a wink in Kai's direction.

"Not a chance!" Jet smiled.

"But no cussing!" Uncle Per boomed out. "Or your mother will kill me!"

"Okay," Jet said. "Are you ready?" She waited for that moment of quiet that comes before a story.

"It was such a perfect day, it would have been a crime not to go sailing."

21

As LUCK WOULD have it, the next day was perfect for sailing—clear, warm, and windy. Jet was lurking in the hall as Kai took his shower, and when he opened the door she said, "Are the patches on the *Saga* cured yet?" She was bouncing on her toes like a little kid.

"No," he said quickly, and turned away.

He closed the door of his room before she could ask him anything else. His heart was hammering as if he'd run up a mountain. He wanted the boat to be fixed and didn't, wanted to sail and dreaded the idea of being on the water. He was ashamed of being rude to his cousin and exasperated with her—what? Her energy was boundless. She wasn't afraid of anything. She was like that girl with the sailor suit in the Shōjo comics. She even had the long blond hair and blue eyes. All she needed was a talking cat and super-powers. The thought of spending another day with her made him want to hide under the covers and sleep until noon.

Ojī-san would want him to be a better man than that. Kai gathered his resolve and headed downstairs.

"Saddle Mountain!" Uncle Per announced as Kai slid into his seat at the breakfast table.

"It'll be great," Jet said. "We can go geocaching!"

"Geocaching?" Kai said.

"It's a treasure hunt," Oliver mumbled, his mouth full of waffles. He was up to his elbows in syrup, as usual. "It's awesome!"

Jet opened up a website and scrolled through some pages. "Look, there's a new cache on the trail on the way up." Jet scribbled down the coordinates. "It's three stars for terrain because the trail is steep, but it's only two stars for difficulty." Jet turned to Oliver. "Do you want to find that one?"

"How big?" Oliver said.

"Medium. Go ask Mom if she's got leftover swag from Comic Con to swap for the treasure."

Oliver scooted off to the living room, where Aunt Karin was already penciling comic-book pages.

"You're supposed to swap something when you find the treasure," Jet said. "I make origami sailboats."

"Are you going to find a harder one for you and Kai?" Uncle Per asked. He popped a fresh waffle out of the iron and slathered on butter and syrup.

Jet clicked around the map on the screen. "Here we go," she said. "A microcache, and it's five out of five stars for difficulty. Want to try it?"

"I guess."

"Haven't you ever done this before? They have caches all over the world." Jet flicked her finger across the screen and zoomed the map to Japan. It was peppered with green squares to mark hidden caches. There were more than a dozen in his home prefecture.

"Geocaches are everywhere," Uncle Per said. "Give it a try. Your dad would like this game. Something to look forward to when you go home."

Kai slid in next to Jet and scrolled around the map. There were treasures hidden all over the world, and he'd never known to look for them.

IN THE CAR Oliver quietly insisted Kai sit next to him. Oliver loved the Naruto comic so much that Kai had gone back and gotten a dozen more the next

day. Now Oliver had a fistful of manga and was determined to discuss every last detail. He wasn't nearly as shy as Kai first guessed. It was kind of cool to see Oliver getting excited about all the same comics Kai loved when he was a little kid.

They parked at the Saddle Mountain trailhead. Jet typed in the coordinates for the easy geocache. Oliver took command of the GPS, even though they had a thousand feet to climb before they'd be close to the hidden treasure box. He picked out a stick to be his quarterstaff or broadsword, as the adventure required. He and Uncle Per spun one hero tale after another as they walked, borrowing equally from Norse myths and Marvel comics. Oliver called out the distance on the GPS as they got closer to the geocache. He anticipated dragons at every turn.

Kai walked up the trail steadily, barely listening to Oliver's unfolding adventure story and grateful Jet didn't feel like talking. He'd taken several pictures at the start and sent them to his father. It felt good to visit a place that meant something to him, and it felt even better to do something that would bring him comfort.

But Kai hadn't expected to be afraid. He didn't know the hills would be so much like the ones above

his hometown. The smell of pine trees was achingly familiar. The ferns that grew along the trail looked exactly the same. The wind made the tall pines rub against each other, making eerie creaking and popping noises. More than the climb made his heart race.

The earthquake made trees dance like this when he was climbing the hills behind his town. He'd seen and heard a hundred things that day he hoped to never remember. The crack of falling trees and the rumble of landslides set off by the aftershocks. The whimpering of a drenched farm dog, faithfully following a half-dozen chickens through the underbrush and stopping every few steps, smelling the ground for a path home. Worst of all was the sound of people wailing, calling encouragement to those trying to wade out of the advancing edges of the tide, gasping and groaning as people sheltering on rooftops were swept away.

Kai was so lost in thought that he barely noticed the excitement building as Oliver got closer and closer to the GPS point where the geocache was hidden. When they were finally on top of the target, Oliver shouted with glee and attacked the sword fern that stood above the treasure as if it were a guarding dragon. Kai flinched as though he'd been struck in the face.

The ground is not moving, he told himself. I am not all alone. Mom and Dad are fine. They are not going to die of radiation. They'll get the reactor fixed. They'll find . . . But he could not tell himself what he'd been repeating every night as he paced the floor trying to wear himself out enough to sleep. It had been a week. They hadn't found new survivors for days.

His father had told him not to give up hope. His grandparents might be in a different survivors' camp. The final list of people who died wouldn't be ready for weeks. Kai clasped his hands together to keep them from shaking. He closed his eyes and tried to remember what Ojī-san told him about meditating. But the only word he could remember was his grandfather's last word—*run*. Why had he listened?

"Kai?"

Oliver slipped his small and sweaty hand into his. The sword stick in Oliver's other hand was still raised to fend off the invisible.

"Only pretend dragons," Oliver said.

He leaned in and rested his head under Kai's chin. Kai froze. He'd never had a brother, never babysat, never hugged someone younger than him. Kai rested his cheek on Oliver's head and watched Jet and his

uncle uncover the treasure—a plastic shoe box with a logbook, a bunch of local postcards, and some Mardi Gras beads.

"I'm too old for dragons," Kai said. "Sorry."

Oliver gave him a quick hug and scampered off to sign his name in the logbook. He took a green strand of beads and left one of Aunt Karin's mini comic books.

The hike got easier after that. Oliver gave Kai the GPS, and Uncle Per explained how to use it. Kai looked for things in the forest that didn't remind him of home. Thimbleberries were new, and chickarees and banana slugs. They climbed up out of the trees to a rocky knob that was the east horn of Saddle Mountain. The trail dipped down, crossed a boulder field, and rose again to a wooden platform on the western horn of the saddle. Their GPS point drew closer as they made the final scramble up to the observation platform.

When they reached the top, Kai gasped at the view of the river and the ocean, but everyone else was intent on finding the geocache. The GPS said it should be in the middle of the platform. But nothing was up there except weathered wooden deck boards, a railing, and a warning sign about not leaving the platform.

"It's a microcache," Jet was saying as she consulted her notebook. "So less than three inches in any dimension. I bet it's one of those magnetic things to hide a key in."

"It's supposed to be right here," Oliver insisted, standing dead center on the platform. He jumped up and down on the spot. "Right here! Right here!"

"Oh, I've got an idea." Jet skipped to the edge of the platform, lay down on her stomach, and hung her head over the edge. "Yes! Metal cross braces."

Oliver joined her. "Lot of spiders down there," he said.

Jet shrugged off the spiders and worked her way under the platform.

"Where do you think you're going?" Uncle Per said. "Get back up here! I'll go."

"It's not dad-size under there," Oliver said.

"It says don't leave the platform." Kai gestured to the sign they were all ignoring. He shook his head in amazement as Jet's feet disappeared under the wooden decking.

"Who's leaving the platform?" came Jet's muffled voice from underneath their feet. "I'm hanging on super tight!"

143

Uncle Per muttered under his breath as he paced from one edge to another.

"Will you relax? If I fall I'm going to fall an entire three inches . . . oof . . . two inches . . . ow! Got it!"

"She got it! She got it!" Oliver began a victory dance.

Jet emerged a few minutes later, fist first. Oliver took the tiny metal key case from her hand, and Uncle Per helped her up. Inside was a single sheet of paper folded many times over and a mini pencil.

"Look, Kai," Oliver said, tugging at his arm. "Somebody from Kobe, Japan! And he wrote in secret code!"

"My kanji is limited to shipping terms," Per said. "What does it say?" He handed over the log.

"Breathtaking," Kai read. He handed the log to Jet. They all signed it, and Kai carefully wrote out the kanji characters for Ikata. Jet returned the cache to its hiding place. Uncle Per broke out the snacks and water bottles. Kai was content to just lean and look, imagining his father looking over the same spot decades ago. He wondered, for the first time, if his father ever missed his hometown.

After a while Uncle Per came over and leaned alongside him.

"There's something I've been wanting to give you ever since you arrived," he said. He took a wooden box out of his pocket.

"This is for you."

Kai opened it. Inside was a round brass thing that looked like a pocket watch with a lid. Jet peered over his shoulder.

"Go on, take it," Uncle Per said.

Kai cradled it in his palm. It was heavier than it looked. There was a cutout in the lid in the shape of a squared-off heart. U.S. ENGINEER CORPS was stamped on the rim.

"It was your great-grandpa's compass," Uncle Per said. "The one he brought back from the First World War. He used it to guide ships over the bar."

The lid opened smoothly. The disk of the compass bobbled. Kai turned to the left and right, watching the north point swing into place. He turned to show Jet, but she'd stepped away. Uncle Per cupped his hand under Kai's. He lifted the compass to eye level.

"You line it up like this, and then look through the sighting hole."

The heart shape on the lid was upside down now, and it looked like an up-pointing arrow. It had a

polished metal mirror underneath that reflected the dial.

"Then you find a way marker to guide you." Uncle Per turned to the north and lined up the compass so Kai could see the Astoria Column through the sighting hole.

"Wow," Kai said. "It's so old, but it still works perfectly."

"Do you like it?"

Without thinking, Kai nodded yes.

"It's yours."

22

JET SLIPPED AWAY from Kai and her dad and went to stand on the far side of the platform. The morning fog had burned off, but the view was lost on her.

She had seen the compass before. She'd snooped in the chest in Dad's office last year. The chest held old woolen pilot uniforms, a brass telescope, coins from all over the world, and war medals. But the compass was the prize of them all. As soon as she'd seen it, she'd wanted it. Her cell phone had a compass app. Sure. But this was the real thing! She'd promised it to herself, promised that she'd earn the right to own it.

Across the platform Dad was taking Kai's picture. Jet felt struck through, as if the future she'd always imagined had run aground. Did he not even think of her as a mariner? Okay, technically she hadn't told him that she wanted to be a pilot, not since she'd made a dramatic pronouncement at Thanksgiving dinner when she was six.

Dad had laughed and acted like she was being cute. Even when she was little, cute was the last thing Jet wanted to be. She'd gone to her closet that night and thrown away everything pink, including socks and underwear. She promised herself he'd never call her cute again. She joined the swim team and won her weight in medals and trophies. She got books from the library about the weather and the ocean and every sea captain she could find. There was one book about an Irish woman sea captain that she'd loved so much, she stole it from the library and read it until the covers fell off.

All she wanted was for him to understand that she was serious about being a pilot. But maybe it was already too late. Maybe he wanted Kai. Piloting was a heritage business, and not just on the Columbia. It was the same on the Mississippi, in San Francisco Bay, on the Chesapeake, everywhere. Dads handed pilotage on to their sons like they'd done for generations.

Jet kicked at the platform railing. Kai could fix a boat. Fine. But he hadn't set eyes on the Columbia

before this summer. He didn't know the name of a single navigation marker. If she could just get out there and win the Treasure Island Race. Dad would respect her then. Everybody would.

She knew that course like nobody else. She could win the thing. The *Saga* could be handled by a single sailor. It would be a challenge to reach the jib sheets from the stern, but Jet was getting taller, she could feel it. She was almost thirteen. Okay, not until September, but she felt thirteen now. Twelve was so tight on her, it itched. She had to persuade him to let her race. She lined up her best arguments. The race was only a month away. She'd need every minute of practice she could get.

Dad was still talking to Kai about the compass. Her great-grandfather's compass. It just wasn't right. It should be hers. She was the one who wanted to be a pilot. Kai hated the ocean.

Jet slumped against the opposite railing and studied her cousin. Oliver came over and started taking pictures of Kai and Dad together. Dad was clowning around like usual, trying to get Kai to laugh. Kai was trying to be all dignified for his father.

Jet sighed. What right did she have to complain?

Kai had lost everything. His parents were making him stay a million miles away, with cousins he didn't know. Meanwhile everybody he knew was in the thick of rescuing his hometown—one heroic inch at a time.

He's like me, Jet thought, or like I would be if I ever came down with a case of good manners. He was only happy when he was fixing the *Saga*. He needed a project, something that would make him feel like he wasn't wasting his summer playing like a little kid.

Jet turned to the northeast, where she could just make out the first few islands in the Treasure Island racecourse. Could she ask him when he was so afraid of the water? But he mended the *Saga* with such care. He did love to sail. Loved it and hated the ocean. It was like a curse straight out of mythology.

23

"WHY ME?" KAI said quietly. He turned to his uncle with the compass in his hand.

"You're an Ellstrom, aren't you?"

"But I don't live here."

"You'll come back," Uncle Per said confidently.

Kai found 260° west by south on the compass—the course home. He'd dreamed of going home night after night, and yet how could he face them when he'd run away? All his friends were going to remember this summer forever. They'd remember the heat, the cramped tents, the work, but more than anything, they'd remember that feeling of solidarity from overcoming something together. For the rest of Kai's life, he'd be outside the circle of those who'd given their all when their town needed them most. No one could come back from that.

"Not so easy to be a boy between cultures, is it?" Uncle Per said.

"No."

His friends at home never said, "You're only half Japanese so we don't like you." But everything came easily to them. Kai was always in doubt. Did he laugh too loud? Answer too many things wrong and make the class look bad? Score too many soccer goals, like a show-off? He was never sure he'd said or done the right thing.

"The sea could be your country," Uncle Per said. "Lots of mariners are like you—a foot in more than one place. Captain a ship, and you're a citizen of the whole world. You come from way-finding people, Kai. You and I go all the way back to the Vikings."

Kai's father had left the navy before he was born, so Kai usually thought of him as just a nuclear engineer, but the truth was that every man in Kai's family had been a mariner of one kind or another.

"Whichever you choose, the sea will always be a home to you," Uncle Per said, and then he left Kai alone with his thoughts.

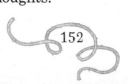

Kai turned west. The ocean was blue and clean and still. The tsunami had been black and loud. It plowed through his town like a bulldozer, pushing cars and boats on the leading edge, dragging garbage and house frames and human bodies behind. He shuddered remembering it.

Kai knew that in the minds of his classmates he'd always be the boy who ran away. But something in him, maybe the American in him, wanted to believe in second chances. Enough to step in a boat and face the ghosts that hovered in the mists between the ocean and the air?

Yes. That much.

He felt the weight of his great-grandfather's compass in his hand. "Generations of seafaring men," Uncle Per had said. Ojī-san's brother and father and grandfather were all fishermen. They'd faced the dark water before. Kai walked over to where his cousin was studying the river.

"Jet," he said. "About that race . . . Do you need a crew?"

24

YESTERDAY IN THE clear sunshine on top of Saddle Mountain, taking Kai as her sailing partner seemed like a brilliant plan, a sure path to the glory of a championship cup. Now in the cold mist of early morning at the sailing club, Jet saw three fatal flaws in her thinking.

One: Kai had apparently never sailed in English before. He kept reverting to Japanese for sailboat parts. It was weird; he spoke English as well as she did. He didn't even have an accent like the Japanese tourists who come off the cruise ships. But he couldn't keep it straight that the *sheet* was the rope that moved the sail from side to side, and the *halyard* was the rope that lifted a sail up and down. Jet had known all this for so long, she couldn't remember not knowing. Sailing in English was going to take some practice.

Problem number two: they hadn't decided who was going to be helmsman and who was going to be crew. The helmsman did the steering and was in command. When she and Beck used to sail together, they traded halfway through the sail. That would be fair. But Beck knew these waters, and Kai didn't. Maybe Kai would be fine with letting her take the helm. Or maybe he'd be ashamed to not be in charge. She'd taken only a quick look at the manga he'd given to Oliver, but it was pretty clear that in Japan, girls were for decoration and not command.

Problem number three: Kai was afraid of the water. What Jet hadn't figured out or, okay, even thought about, was how she was going to help him get over his fear. The whole time they were rigging up the boat, Kai wouldn't even look at the water. How was he going to cope with the current and waves on the Columbia? The main job of the crew, besides handling the jib sail, was to keep an eye on the water so they didn't crash into anything.

They wheeled the *Saga* down from the garage. Jet

would just have to help him get over all that. The thing to do with a fear was to charge right through it. The thrill of overcoming what scared you was totally worth the agony.

Jet and Kai stopped the boat trailer at the edge of the water. He untied the ropes, and Jet waded into the water behind the boat.

"Come on!" she called to Kai.

He stayed on the boat ramp.

"I need a hand here," Jet said.

Kai stayed rooted to his spot.

"I can't pull the boat off the trailer all by myself."

Kai walked toward the water and stopped an inch before the spot where the water would touch his feet. He took the side rails of the *Saga* and shoved the boat toward Jet. She staggered a few steps backward as it slipped easily into Youngs Bay.

"Thanks!" Jet said. She took the bowline and tied it off to the dock.

"Well, are you ready?" she asked, still knee-deep in water.

Kai didn't answer.

"I checked the tide. I swear."

Kai stood there frozen, staring at Jet and the blue-green water around her legs.

"We've got two good hours left before the tide turns. Let's get out there!" Jet reached down, scooped a handful of water, and tossed it at Kai. He flinched as though she were attacking him.

"Oh, come on, Kai. It's just water."

Beck would have splashed her right back. Kai was just as much an Ellstrom as her. Where was his fight? He just needed to try. Jet kicked a larger splash at him, and then another.

"Get out here!" she called.

It was hot. The water felt great. He was going to have an awesome time. All he had to do was try, but he was just standing there, not saying no, but not saying yes, either. Jet grabbed the bailer from the *Saga* and scooped up a whole quart of water.

"Are you chicken?"

"No."

"Don't you want to sail?"

"Yes."

"Well get out here then!"

Jet heaved the water at Kai. The instant the water

157

left the bailer, she knew she was wrong. Knew this was the cruelest thing she'd ever done. And she'd done it to the one boy who didn't deserve it.

Kai didn't move. He didn't run. Didn't even flinch, but he braced for the impact of the water like a man facing the executioner's ax. The water flew in a sparkling blue arc and drenched Kai from head to foot. He shuddered, looked for a moment like he might throw up, and then turned away without a word.

"Kai?"

Jet dropped the bailer, flooded with shame. Roland did things like this, not her.

Kai walked away from the marina and back up to the main road. He didn't look back.

"Kai, wait!"

He broke into a run. Jet jogged after him, but he was taller and soon left her in the dust. Stopping at the bridge, Jet leaned against the railing to catch her breath.

Kai wanted to sail. And he was refusing to get wet. A real captain would know what to say to her crew. Jet had no idea. She turned around and trudged back to the marina, where the *Saga* was still bobbing in the water, Kai's patches holding beautifully.

She should practice solo. It would do her good. She pulled the jib sheet over where she could reach it easily and headed into the bay. The wind was steady. She made her first tack and then another. She trimmed the sail for maximum speed, but that lift she always felt when the wind swelled her sails just wasn't there. She'd done the wrong thing, and her cousin was gone.

The water had a welcoming sparkle. The wind was perfect. Gulls swooped low over her sail, cheering her on, but there was no joy. Jet turned her boat toward shore. It took her more than an hour to load the boat onto its trailer by herself. By the time she'd put the boat away and biked all the long way home, she was hot and tired and sunburned and sad. Mostly sad.

25

KAI'S FIRST DAY of silence was like a drink of cold water when you're dying of thirst. It was an easy enough choice; he never wanted to talk to Jet again. He didn't want to tattle on her. Didn't want an apology. He shouldn't have to explain himself. She should know that his grandparents were lost somewhere in the Pacific. How could she expect him to wade in, as if their lives meant nothing to him? No. He just wanted the peace of not having to deal with her at all.

At first Uncle Per didn't even notice. He told one of his sea stories at dinner. Kai smiled and nodded in all the spots he was supposed to. Jet peppered Uncle Per with questions, and nobody noticed that Kai wasn't talking—except Oliver.

Oliver stopped talking, too. After dinner he took

Kai by the hand and set up the chessboard on the rug while Uncle Per read *The Three Musketeers* aloud. Jet made her excuses, and Aunt Karin drew comics in her work corner.

The next morning, instead of struggling to swallow the Froot Loops and Count Chocula, Kai went to the garden and picked some peas and another green leafy thing that looked tasty. Not quite what he needed for proper miso soup, but as soon as he could figure out where to buy miso and seaweed, he'd be all set. On summer days like this, Ojī-san used to meditate in Obā-san's garden. Kai tried to remember what his grandfather had said about meditating. Sit mindfully. Breathe slowly.

Kai heard Jet come charging out of the house. She was going to demand an explanation. Kai closed his eyes, but his blood was boiling. Who did she think she was? She'd never lost anything. He listened to her coming closer, through the little stand of pear trees. He braced himself for conflict, but Jet stopped a good ways off. Kai was determined not to answer her, no matter what she said. But instead of the flood of demands he was expecting, she just stood there, as silent as him.

And then she turned and walked away. On tiptoe. Kai didn't think Jet knew how.

The rest of the morning was perfect. Kai tended the garden while Jet mowed the grass. She worked with her head down, not talking. When Aunt Karin asked them to go to the farmers' market, Jet made an excuse to stay home. She didn't even look at him.

Just by luck, he and Aunt Karin found a tiny stall in the market run by a Russian woman. She had mushrooms and daikon radishes and homemade pickles. She'd set out samples. Kai could have happily eaten every pickle on the plate. They weren't exactly like Obā-san's pickles, but the familiar salty sourness of them filled him up in a way ten milk shakes never would.

The silence continued at lunch. Jet pushed her macaroni around with her fork but didn't actually swallow any of it. After lunch she went to the barn. There was peace in the house for hours. Eventually Kai decided to join Oliver, who was watching TV in the living room while Aunt Karin inked her comic-book panels. But Oliver took off the minute Kai sat down.

"Did you and Oliver have an argument?" Aunt Karin said.

162

Kai shook his head.

It was an honest answer. Sort of.

Outside the window they could see Oliver at the edge of the orchard. He picked up a stick and swung it like a bat at the pears. In a few minutes every pear in his reach was on the ground. It was odd. Oliver adored combat like nobody Kai had ever known, but he wasn't destructive. Aunt Karin gave Kai a searching look, and Kai had the distinct feeling he should say something to her, but silence was easy and he was weary of trying.

26

THE THIRD SATURDAY in June was the annual sand-castle contest, and ever since she was seven, Jet had gone to Cannon Beach with Bridgie and Skye and all three of Bridgie's grandmothers for a day of building stuff in the sand. After her first disastrous attempt to sail with Kai, a day at the beach would be a relief. Jet owed her cousin an apology. She wanted to apologize, but he wouldn't talk to her, wouldn't even look at her, and she didn't know how to start. The minute the big blue grandma truck pulled up, Jet bolted out the door without a backward look.

Jet had flunked crayons in kindergarten, so she always let Skye and Bridgie design their castle. Bridgie launched into the plan before Jet had even buckled up.

"I was totally going to go for the tallest castle yet," Bridgie said, sketch pad in hand.

"Like the one that collapsed on us last time?" Skye said.

"We're not in the little-kid competition anymore," Jet added. Not that she cared so much about winning when it came to sand castles. Still, she didn't want to look like an idiot.

"You're in the Sand Teen division now," Grandma Abby chirped. Grandma Bernice was already taking pictures of them in the backseat.

"Right! I know!" Bridgie said. "We need a theme this year. So important."

"A theme?" Skye said, skeptically. "Is that required?"

"No, but you're going to love it," Bridgie said. "Trust me."

Jet obliged her with a drum roll.

"Starfish!" Bridgie announced.

"You mean sea stars?" Skye said. She'd done a project about them in school.

"Right! Sea stars. We'll call it the *Mystery of the Missing Starfish*." Bridgie flipped open her sketchbook. Skye and Jet leaned in.

"Wow," Skye said. "Can we do this?"

"Oh yes!" Grandma Claire said from the driver's seat. "People do special causes all the time: spotted owls, honoring veterans, global warming." She went on and on with the list of causes she remembered from years past. Grandma Claire's truck was covered in bumper stickers. Jet had gotten used to being honked at in her truck.

Bridgie's sketch showed a tide pool full of sea urchins, mussels, and barnacles. A giant starfish climbed out of the tide pool, and as it crawled away it got smaller and legs fell off until it finally melted away into the sand. Sea stars had been dying from a wasting disease all down the Oregon coast. It was terrible. Their bodies rotted into a gooey mush. Skye had talked about it for months. She had a soft spot for lost causes.

"This is awesome, Bridgie," Jet said. "Plus the tide pool isn't tall enough to crumble."

"You haven't even seen the best part," Bridgie said. She took out a clipboard with flyers. "It's a baby sea-star register." She handed it to Skye. "You can talk to people about sea stars and how to be a citizen scientist all day long if you want."

"You're the best, Bridgie!" Skye said.

The two of them bickered about the design the rest of the way to Cannon Beach. Jet didn't mind. She loved it when her friends cared about cool things, not just malls and makeup, but things that really mattered. All her bad feelings about splashing Kai started to fade.

When they got to the beach, they unpacked Grandma Abby's amazing collection of sand-sculpting tools and Grandma Bernice's equally amazing cooler of star-shaped sandwiches. It was chilly when they started building, but digging in the sand soon warmed them up. They had four hours until judging, and five until the tide washed their work away.

The first hour of the contest, the beach was empty except for other builders. Grandma B launched into her usual role as the paparazzo. Grandmas A and C lounged and read books. Jet and Skye brought sand and water wherever Bridgie needed them and shaped the rough outlines. Bridgie followed after with the sculpting tools and a spray bottle of water. They decorated the tide pool with a bunch of mussel shells and sea-urchin skeletons and dead barnacles.

"So, Skye," Bridgie said as they were finishing up, "did you tell Jet your news?"

"News?" Jet turned to Skye. When she spent every

school day with them, there was never news she missed. Last summer and all the summers before, when she and Beck built stuff together, she hadn't minded being out of the loop, but something about the way Bridgie said *news* made her stomach twist.

"What's going on?" Jet said.

"Well . . ." Skye was not shy about speaking up. Jet loved that about her, but suddenly she looked like a little kid called up to read a book report.

"It's okay," Jet said. "What's up?"

"Well," Skye said again.

"Oh, just tell her!" Bridgie set down her sand tools for the first time in three hours. She was bursting with the news, a ridiculous grin on her face. She brushed off her hands and pulled out the sandwiches and sodas.

"So a bunch of us were down at the skate park yesterday," Skye went on. "And Roland and I got to talking because we have all the same music on our phones and—"

"They're going out!" Bridgie barged in.

"Out?" Jet looked from one friend to the other.

"Yes," Sky said blushing like a beet.

"It's *so* cute!" Bridgie said.

Are you kidding me? was Jet's first thought. She took a huge bite of sandwich so she wouldn't say it aloud. *Couldn't this wait until high school?* was her second thought—also better not said out loud. And then it really hit her.

"Wait a minute. Roland?" Jet said. "Roland from school?"

Roland the name caller, she thought. Roland the snob. Roland the colossal toadstool. She took several more bites to keep from saying all this. Roland the stealer of friends.

"Of course," Skye said. "What other Roland is there?"

"He gave her an otter!" Bridgie went on.

"A toy otter," Skye said. "It's cute."

"Oh," Jet said, still trying to wrap her head around the idea. "Because sea otters are endangered, and you care about endangered animals. Right?"

"It's *so* cute!" Bridgie cooed.

"Cute? Cute! What's the matter with you two!" Jet said. "Why him?"

Last fall, when Roland had started calling her Spot, Skye and Bridgie persuaded every girl in class,

and the school librarian, to draw freckles on their faces with eyeliner. They used to be on her side. Jet felt like she'd taken a wrong tack and lost the wind.

"Because he asked me," Skye said.

"That's not a reason," Jet said.

"Just because he teased you last year doesn't make him a monster," Skye said. She looked down at Jet. Skye was so much taller that looking down was a regular thing, but Jet had never felt small beside her friend before.

"We should have a code," Bridgie said enthusiastically. "A boyfriend code. We have to be nice to each other's boyfriends." She looked to Skye for an approving nod. "And our boyfriends have to be nice to all of us."

"We don't have boyfriends," Jet said.

Bridgie shot her a look. It was the wrong thing to say. The knot in Jet's stomach tightened.

"Yet," Jet said quickly. "Not yet."

"Here they come," Skye said, pointing up the beach. Roland and Beck and all three of the Mikes were headed their way. Skye and Bridgie stood up and waved. They brushed off their sand.

"You don't have to be his girlfriend," Jet said

quickly. "You could say you were kidding. Please. I don't trust him."

Jet wracked her brains to figure out what Skye saw in him. What everyone saw in him. He said mean things with a laugh and everyone laughed with him, as if being funny made it okay to be mean. It wasn't just her, and it wasn't just teasing. He was awful to the boy who liked to sew and to the girl who stuttered.

"You're not being fair," Bridgie said. "He can be nice."

Not to everybody, Jet thought.

"I don't want to fight about this," Skye said.

"Fine," Jet said. "Go. I'll just stay here because I care about sea otters—real sea otters. And sea stars. I'll just take this." She picked up the clipboard with its flyers about tracking the health of baby sea stars. "And I'll sign people up to be citizen scientists." Jet took a deep breath. She faked a smile.

"Go on, girls," Grandma Abby said gently. "We'll hang out with Jet for a while."

Jet breathed a huge sigh of relief when Skye and Bridgie ran off to meet the boys. She didn't want to

face them—not today, maybe not ever. She'd driven her only cousin away, and now she didn't have a friend left.

"Plenty of other fish in the sea," Grandma Claire announced. As if this were about Jet wanting a boyfriend of her own.

"Who needs a fish?" Grandma Bernice said. "Slippery old things." She went on for quite a while with the fish metaphor, and then Grandmas A through C started saying things about . . . well . . . "fish" that old ladies should not say out loud. They all found it hilarious. Jet wanted to curl up and bury herself in the sand. By the time awards rolled around, she was fresh out of fake smile, and even the blue ribbon didn't make a difference.

27

Kᴀɪ ᴡᴀꜱ ᴛʜʀɪʟʟᴇᴅ to see Jet take off with her friends for the beach. He spent most of the day with Uncle Per, culling spoiled fruit from the trees and weeding the garden. He'd missed the familiar work of tending his *obā-san*'s herbs and flowers.

That night at dinner, Uncle Per didn't have any stories to tell. Jet didn't say anything, either, and Oliver was a turtle in his shell. The silence gave him plenty of time to think. Into that quiet came the memory of Obā-san's words when one of the bigger boys had thrown rocks at him on the way home from school. *"Makenaide. Gambare,"* she'd said. "Carry on."

"Gambare!" the boys shouted during a soccer match when anyone showed a moment of weakness. "Toughen up!" "Keep going!" He'd heard it all his life. The book

his uncle was reading was a very Japanese kind of story, with court rivals and spies and plenty of fighting. And that thing d'Artagnan said—"All for one and one for all"—that was the sort of thing his grandfather would say, or his principal.

It was a value he was falling short on. Jet had done a coldhearted thing, but he had responded just as coldly. He should apologize.

He didn't have to guess where Jet went after dinner. She had this crazy habit of sitting on the porch roof. Kai's bedroom was right next to hers. He slid open his window and sat on the roof beside her. Jet had binoculars in her hand. Kai could hear marine radio coming from her room. Even though it was after nine o'clock, the sun still cast long shadows across the garden. A ship worked its way over the bar and up the Columbia. Kai thought about what he wanted to say. After two and a half days of saying nothing, he wanted to get it right.

"I'm sorry," Jet blurted out. "I knew you were afraid of the water, and I splashed you anyway. That was wrong. I shouldn't have done it."

"That's okay—" Kai began, but Jet cut him off.

"It's not okay. It was mean," she said. She kept

her eyes fixed on the bar and the ship moving across it. "When I'm afraid of something, I jump anyway. I don't know why. I'm just like that. I wanted to help you get over it, and now I probably made it worse." Jet wrapped her arms around her knees and rested her chin on them.

"No," Kai said, still scrambling for the right thing to say.

Jet drove him crazy, even when she wasn't being mean, but at least she'd been trying to help. In all his silence Kai had only been serving himself. His grandparents had taught him better. Maybe if he conquered his fears. Maybe if he crewed faithfully for his cousin, then his grandparents would be found. Even if it was only their bodies recovered, it would bring his mother peace to give them a proper funeral.

"I hate being afraid," Kai said. "I want to get over it."

"You don't have to," Jet said. "I was wrong to push you."

"But *I* want to push me," Kai said. "Everyone at home is doing brave things, hard things, every day, and I'm just . . ." He scraped his palms along the rough shingles of the roof so the sting would help him not

cry. He had to do something, be something, they could respect.

"Maybe it's too soon," Jet said.

"I want to sail." He curled his hands into fists. *Gambare.* No matter what the cost. "For my family," he said.

"We can be on the water without going in," Jet said. "I promise I'll never push you again."

"Deal," Kai said.

And then they sat in a silence that wasn't uncomfortable at all. The sun sank over the water, lighting up the clouds in pink and orange. Jet passed him the binoculars and pointed to the ship that had just cleared the bar and was heading out to sea.

"That one's going to Yokohama," Jet said. "Carrying timber for new houses."

Kai followed it with the binoculars until the ship's lights disappeared over the horizon, and the sky was freckled with stars.

28

THE NEXT MORNING Jet and Kai tried again. It was that stillest moment of the day, before the wind picked up and right at the turn of the tide. The water of Youngs Bay was a sheet of glass. Gray herons that fished on the edges of the bay took off low across the water. Their slow, rowing wing beats stirred the morning fog into swirls. A bald eagle soared overhead, looking for running salmon. It was Jet's favorite time of day, but she could see that the beauty was lost on Kai.

The kind thing would be to let him off the hook. But it was too late for that. Kai promised to race. No way was he going to back out. He'd die trying. To be honest, he looked a little bit like he was dying right in front of her. His voice went all breathy like hers did before oral reports in school. Fine. If Kai was all in, Jet was, too.

They'd have a slack current for the first part of their sail. She'd walk him through it one step at a time.

And then Beck and Roland showed up. It was bad enough they had to practice in the same bay. They could at least practice at a different time. Kai recognized Beck from before. He walked right over and started talking to the enemy! Maybe he missed having boys his age to hang out with. They stood in a ring around the *Viking,* and Kai asked one question after another, all smiles.

"Hey," Jet said twenty minutes later, when she'd completely exhausted any pretense of busywork on the *Saga.* "Ready to get out there?"

The boys turned in unison.

"The tide," she said. "It's turning. We should sail."

"Look, it's got a toe strap," Kai said. "So they can lean over the side without falling out, if the wind is strong enough to make the boat ride up on one hull."

Great, Jet thought. Another feature maximizing their speed. She stole a look at the sleek twin hulls. She was going to have to work harder than she'd ever worked before to beat this boat.

"And the sail," Kai went on eagerly. "Just over a hundred square feet."

"Awesome," Jet said frostily.

The mast was taller than hers. Winning was going to take more than work. She was going to need every ounce of luck she could get.

"Got your work cut out for you!" Roland said, way more cheerfully than he needed to. "We're gonna smoke you come race day."

Beck dug a hole in the dirt with his sneaker. He didn't take Roland's side, but he didn't take Jet's, either. And Kai just stood there smiling away, as if family honor wasn't at stake.

"Oh yeah?" Jet said, looking from Roland to Beck.

Maybe sabotage was the solution. Jet entertained a brief fantasy involving a dark night and an ax. No, there'd be no victory in that. Besides, Beck loved that boat, and maybe, just maybe, it would give him a way to sail with his dad again. But the championship at the regatta? No way was she giving that up, not to a couple of video-game-playing skateboarders.

"Prove it!" Jet said. She turned on her heel and went to the dock to launch the *Saga*.

The last of the morning fog rose off the bay. Kai hesitated before getting in the boat. He closed his eyes as the mist swirled along the ground and disappeared

into the tall grasses. He shivered but then opened his eyes, squared his shoulders, and got into the boat.

"Ready?" Jet said.

"Un," Kai said crisply. "Let's go."

Jet pushed off, hopped into the stern, and sat at the tiller. Kai pushed the daggerboard down into the water, and Jet lowered the rudder. She took them on an easy tack across the bay to give Kai some time to settle in. He was stronger than Oliver by a mile, so he handled the jib sail a lot faster. He was taller, too, so if she needed him to hold the tiller steady, he'd be able to reach, no problem. Once they really got into a groove of sailing together, they'd be unbeatable! Jet noticed with considerable satisfaction that it took Beck and Roland longer to launch their larger boat and raise its sails because they kept arguing about how to do it right.

Her moment of smugness was brief. Once they were out on the water, Beck and Roland swooped past the *Saga* in a single tack.

Jet saw an opening where she could get ahead of the *Viking* without cutting her off in a way that would disqualify them from a race for failing to yield.

"Ready about," she called.

"Ready," Kai answered, but he was slow to turn the jib, and clumsy.

Jet was an inch from yelling at him to hurry up when she remembered how hard all this was for him. His delay put them directly behind the catamaran, where it would be even harder to pass them on the next tack. Jet dropped back. She kept an eagle eye on the wind and waited for an advantage. When she saw one she called for a turn, and again Kai hesitated. They fell into place directly behind Beck's boat. The worst place to be in a race. As the sun rose higher, the wind picked up, and the *Viking* with its taller sail had the clear advantage.

As they pulled away Roland called over his shoulder, "Hey, Jet, you sail like a girl!"

Jet gripped the tiller so hard, every one of her knuckles popped. If looks could kill, the *Viking* would be going down in flames.

"Don't you worry," Jet said to Kai. "We'll catch them."

29

BUT JET AND Kai didn't catch the *Viking*. Not all morning long. A couple of times when the wind slacked off or got fluky, the *Saga* had the advantage. Jet could have caught them, would have, if Kai had been quicker. He sat in the bow, hunched over like a vulture, eyes darting over the water as if he expected to be swallowed by sea monsters. Jet had muttered more swear words under her breath in the last three hours than she had in her entire life. She could beat the *Viking*, she knew it! Size wasn't everything. She had more experience than Roland, and she was a better judge of the wind than Beck. If only she'd been sailing solo.

The sun climbed high in the sky, and the wind slacked off as it usually did around noon. The *Viking* turned for the shore. In her head Jet could hear the boys congratulating themselves on a race already won. It galled her to pull in beside that bragger Roland. But they'd lose the wind if they stayed out, and her dad was watching from one of the picnic tables. He was taking notes on her nautical judgment, Jet was sure of it. She swallowed her pride and turned for shore.

When they tied up, Kai hopped out and congratulated Beck and Roland on a good sail. They slapped him on the back like boys do and asked him to hang out at the skate park later. Jet wondered for a moment if Kai was a spy for the enemy. She got wearily out of the *Saga* and checked the patches on her hull. They'd held up just fine. She went over every aging bit of her boat. The ropes were in good shape, but the pins that held the rudder in place were worn and should be replaced. She bailed out the water that had splashed into the boat. That was another thing a catamaran sailor didn't have to worry about, taking on water. Jet sighed. Or a nervous crew.

She just didn't understand him. On the first tack they'd taken, Kai had been everything she'd hoped he'd be: fast, strong, and willing to follow her command. But then Beck and Roland got out there, and he went

all cautious. It was like he wanted to lag behind. No, that wasn't fair. He was trying the best he could after all he'd been through.

The boys trailered their boat and went home with Captain Chandler. Dad and Oliver took off for the library, leaving Jet and Kai alone. Jet knew she should say something captain-like and reassuring.

"Next time," she said, forcing cheer into her voice. "We'll be a little faster next time."

"Yes," Kai said. He was grinning more broadly than he had any reason to. "And the time after that and the time after that."

Well, at least he was willing to practice, Jet thought.

"Does the wind come up again in the evening?" Kai asked.

Jet nodded.

"When's the next rising tide?"

"7:42 tonight."

"So almost two hours before sundown," Kai said. "We'll start our real training then."

"Real training?"

Kai looked over his shoulder to make sure Beck and Roland were really gone.

"Yes," he said with determination. "Because now

we know that even though their sail is taller, we have slightly more sail area with our two sails combined. We know two sails are going to be an advantage when the wind is light. And we know that Beck is not a great judge of the wind. And we know that Roland is a rank beginner—enthusiastic but reckless. And we know that they tend to turn early when there's a dozen more feet of sailing room, which means you and I will gain time on every tack if we make longer tacks than they do."

Jet's mouth had fallen open five sentences ago.

"Are you following this?"

She nodded, rethinking her entire calculation of her sailing partner.

"And all they know," Kai said with undisguised glee, "is that we are not very good at sailing a boat." He folded his arms across his chest and grinned in satisfaction. "I bet they hardly practice at all after this."

"You!" Jet sputtered. "You!" She grabbed a float cushion and whacked Kai over the head with it. "You did all that on purpose?" She swiped at him again. "Would it kill you to tell me about this ahead of time!"

"You played it perfectly!" Kai said, ducking the float cushion as it came in for a third blow. "Can't you

185

see it? The more you got mad about falling behind, the more smug Roland got."

Jet paused mid-attack. It couldn't be true. No way.

"You are like rocket fuel for his boys-are-better-than-girls engine," Kai said.

"Am not!" Jet said automatically, but already she was thinking.

"It's okay," Kai said. "You played right into our strategy."

"Our strategy?!" Jet said, voice rising. "You mean the strategy you didn't tell me about?"

"Subtlety is not really your best thing, Jet."

"I can be subtle!" Jet hollered.

Kai turned away. His shoulders were shaking with laughter. Jet whacked him over the head one more time with the boat cushion. But not very hard.

"Fine, Mr. Espionage, you can be subtle for both of us." She dropped the cushion back in the boat. "Just so long as I get to be right!"

"You handle the navigation," Kai said. "Just leave the strategy to me."

"So we train twice a day," Jet said. "But if Beck and Roland are on the water with us, we make them believe we're not very good."

"We have to convince them the *Saga* is nothing but a leaky bathtub."

"And then?"

"Come race day—surprise attack!" Kai said.

"Oh yeah, I'm in."

Jet gave her cousin a hard look. He had been afraid out there, especially right at the very start, when the mist was blowing off the water. But he stuck it out with her for three whole hours. For some reason that Jet was never going to understand, he found something to like about Roland and Beck. Okay, fine. It was probably lonely to not have guys his age to hang out with. But even so, he'd spent the last three hours plotting to beat his new friends in the race. Whatever his reasons, Kai wanted this win maybe even more than she did, and he was willing to work all summer to get there. Jet could not remember meeting a person who seemed more different from her. And now when she least expected it, he was just like her: pride and loyalty above all else.

"One more thing," Jet said. "I want to memorize the river. A month from now I want to know every inch of the course by heart, every current, every ripple."

Every way-finding marker, every depth and sounding,

Jet said to herself. Everything she'd need on her pilot's exam someday. Kai trusted her to captain the race, knowing she'd made a terrible mistake once. He knew the worst the ocean could do, and he got out on the water with her anyway. It was the best present she'd ever been given.

"The charts are in the barn. Will you help me study?"

"Yes."

"Now about that bathtub!" Jet said with a laugh. "Are you calling my *Saga* names?"

"Kidding!" Kai said, throwing up his hands. "I was being subtle. Seriously—you should try it sometime."

"Our *Saga*," Jet charged on, "is the most worthy! The most winning! The best craft of her class! The strongest—"

"She's our legacy," Kai said quietly. "I won't let you down."

30

TWO WEEKS LATER, at sunrise, Kai noticed with satisfaction the rows of calluses on his hands, the blackened thumbnail he'd gotten while lowering the daggerboard at top speed, and the new crop of sun freckles. Out of habit he got out his phone and thumbed through the news. The earthquake was no longer a front-page story, even in Japan. He had to flick through a dozen other stories before he found it. But when he read the headline, his heart skipped a beat. It was the official register of those lost and declared dead.

Kai knew this day would come. His mother had said it would be soon, had sounded almost relieved that it was coming. And now here it was in black and white on the unblinking screen, his grandparents' names, side by side, as they had been in life.

A flood of memories washed over him, a thousand details of sound and smell. He used to sleep on Ojī-san's back porch in the summer. He'd lie very still, waiting for the first sliver of sun to rise above the water. On a calm morning the first rays of sunlight made a golden road across the ink blue of the Uwa Sea.

Kai took the compass out of his pocket. It fit perfectly in his palm. He loved the cool, smooth weight of it. His *ojī-san* had a box of tools for building wooden boats: planes, chisels, rasps, and saws in many shapes and sizes. The wooden handles of the tools had turned from nut brown to almost black over years of use. Ojī-san had said the tools would be Kai's one day. They'd planned to make a wooden boat together, and Kai had loved the idea of spending his whole life in that little house on the bay, making boats with his grandfather.

He flipped up the lid of the compass and waited for the golden arrow to settle on north. He'd already set the sliding marker at 260° west by south to mark the direction home. He wanted to go. It was a solid ache in him that never went away, but the town he knew was gone. He held on to the image of those summer sunrises and the sound of Obā-san lighting the stove

and stirring miso paste into hot water for the morning soup.

Kai wandered into the garden and picked himself a handful of peas and a few leaves of something that smelled good. He couldn't bring his grandparents back or fix Ojī-san's house. He couldn't find or mend the *Ushio-maru*. He couldn't fix anything—except maybe a proper soup for breakfast.

Back in the kitchen, Aunt Karin was packing cookies in boxes. Kai asked if he could use the leftover noodles from the Thai restaurant Uncle Per had taken them to the night before. She showed him the broth in the cupboard that smelled and tasted nothing like broth. It wasn't going to be his grandmother's miso soup, not by a million miles, but with the herbs and peas from the garden, it wasn't so bad. It was better than all that crunchy stuff in boxes that his cousins ate in the morning. He'd just slurped down the last savory noodle when Jet bounded down the stairs and barged into the kitchen.

She was wearing a dress, a blue dress that went down past her knees, with a yellow apron and a vest thing on top. There was a ring of daisies on her head.

It was like she stepped out of a storybook from a hundred years ago.

"If you laugh I'm going to hit you with something large and heavy," Jet said. She slid in next to him at the table and started wolfing down cereal.

"Did I laugh?" Kai said, edging away just in case. "I didn't say anything."

Aunt Karin pulled up a chair behind Jet and started working her tangled hair into braids. Jet went from pale to angry pink to volcano red by the time her mom was done.

Oliver arrived in the kitchen next, wearing dress pants, Sunday shoes, and a bright-red vest with silver buttons. Uncle Per emerged from the garage in full Viking attire.

"So!" Uncle Per said, turning slowly in the kitchen to model his costume for Kai. "There's a spare cape out there. You want to dress up for the festival?"

Kai froze in his seat, horrified.

"No?" Uncle Per laughed. "Not even a helmet with horns?"

Kai shook his head, still speechless.

"Not surprised," Uncle Per boomed out. "Your dad was never one for dressing up, either." He gestured for

Kai to get up and help him carry things out to the car. "Not that I ever gave Lars much of a choice in the matter." He laughed again.

Kai trailed after Uncle Per with an armload of cookie boxes. Kai's father hated bullies above everything, and Kai was beginning to understand how he came by that sentiment.

"Next summer," Uncle Per said, sliding a folding table into the back of the van, "you can help me put together a display for the festival about the ancient navigators of the Pacific."

He paused and gave Kai a meaningful look. Kai was still back on the breezy mention of his return next summer. As if his coming to America was going to be a regular thing.

"Because the Chinese invented the . . ." Uncle Per paused for Kai to fill in the blank.

Kai's thoughts raced. There was a brief mention in the news that the power plant where his parents worked would close for good. They hadn't said it was a done deal, but they wouldn't. Not on the news. Not until long after all the workers knew.

"The compass," Kai said absently. "The Chinese invented the compass."

193

Were his parents thinking of leaving Japan? Would they move back here? They'd never have left Japan while his grandparents were alive. Never.

"But the Chinese used the compass mostly for fortune-telling," Kai added. His father scorned fortune-tellers, and usually Kai did, too, but today he'd have given every penny in his pocket for some hint of what his future held.

"Bet the Japanese got a hold of the early compass and engineered the heck out of it," Uncle Per said. "Do you think?"

Kai shrugged, bewildered by far more than the question. Oliver bounded out of the house, took a couple of skips around the driveway, and launched himself into his usual spot in the van. Jet and Aunt Karin followed. Jet had more boxes of cookies, and Aunt Karin had a bagful of paints and brushes and little pots of glitter.

"Schedule?" Aunt Karin said.

"First performance at ten, and then we have the Midsummer Pole dance at three, and then nothing until our last show at five o'clock," Jet rattled off.

"Great, and do you have your—"

"Phone!" Jet said, pulling hers out of the apron pocket.

"Good. The fairgrounds aren't all that big," Aunt Karin went on, turning to Kai. "You won't get lost. If you need me, I'll be at the booth for the women's shelter selling cookies in the morning, and then I'll be painting faces in the little-kid area in the afternoon. Per will be with the Vikings all day long." She laughed. "You won't have any trouble finding him."

Aunt Karin put some cash for lunch in Kai's hand. "There'll be plenty of kids your age to hang out with, or you can come paint faces with me if you like."

"I'll take pictures for my father," Kai said.

"Oh, he'd love that. Did you know that vest on Oliver is the one your dad used to wear when he danced at the festival?"

"Really?"

Kai's father hardly mentioned being Swedish-American. For sure he never talked about dancing.

"You should hear those boys talk about it. Made to dance with girls!" Aunt Karin said. "In public!"

"The horror!" Jet added.

"Does Oliver mind?" Kai asked.

"You'd think," Aunt Karin said, "shy as he is. But he loves it. You'll see."

"He only started loving it after Dad showed him the part of the book where Captain Hornblower dances a quadrille," Jet said. "Now he thinks it's a form of combat."

"Well, it's no wonder the way *you* dance, honey."

"Mom!" Jet glared at her mother. "I only knocked that boy down one time. One! And it was two years ago!" She turned and looked out the window. "He totally deserved it," she mumbled.

THE FAIRGROUND WAS only a mile away. Kai made himself busy at the start by helping Aunt Karin set out the cookies at the booth for the women's shelter. Then he helped Uncle Per set up a display about Viking navigation. Eventually it was time for his cousins to dance, and to Kai's surprise Oliver really did look like he was having a good time.

Afterward Oliver went off to the Viking tent with Uncle Per. A couple of girls from Jet's school joined the two of them. They wandered around the display tables together, buying snacks and chatting.

The booths had foods Kai had never seen before,

smells he'd never smelled, mysteriously milky soups, and sausages shining with grease. Fortunately there were lots of spicy little fishes, so he had no trouble filling up a plate. There was a storyteller in the library corner wearing a dress like Jet's, but she was his *obā-san*'s age. She had a group of kids under a spell with a story about a Viking ship. Kai's grandmother loved to tell stories, and not just the ghost stories she favored while doing the dishes. She made sure Kai knew his history.

And yet here was a history he knew nothing about. There were booths with toy trolls and pots of lingonberry jam and wreaths woven from wheat and folded paper stars. He took pictures of it all. His father talked about his time in the navy, but he never told stories about his heritage. As Kai walked through the festival, he met dozens of people who remembered Lars and gave Kai messages of encouragement for him to pass along.

Kai wandered outside and sat on the grass alone. He had dozens of pictures ready, but he couldn't quite make himself hit Send. Pictures of Ikata, even Ikata in ruins, made Kai's throat ache. Even now, when he knew for sure his grandparents were gone, he still

wanted to go and put his feet on the ground where they'd stood. Maybe these pictures would make his father want to come back to the United States, even if the power plant didn't close. Maybe he didn't talk about his heritage because he got that awful feeling in his gut that Kai got whenever someone asked him about his hometown. Maybe he felt as rootless in Japan as Kai felt in America. Kai weighed his sense of duty about sending the pictures against how desperately he wanted to go home.

He scrolled through the photos again and deleted every single one.

31

ON THE MORNING of the race, Kai was up with the sun. A week and a half ago, he and Aunt Karin had found a Korean grocer who carried miso paste and the good kind of tofu. Kai gathered greens and carrots from the garden and set out to make the perfect miso soup for his captain. Something easy to eat on a nervous stomach but with plenty of energy for the long hours ahead on the water.

Kai and Jet had been out on the bay every single morning. They'd sailed in every version of wind from a light breeze to a near gale. They'd walked the shoreline of the race and taken kayaks around all the islands. Kai spent hours going over every inch of the *Saga,* replacing every worn cleat and shackle and stay. Jet pitched in on repairs where she could, but more often she pulled up an empty bucket in the boat shed and copied out the chart of the Columbia River, reciting the names of all twenty islands and every navigational marker. They'd sized up the other teams that practiced on Youngs Bay. They speculated wildly about the out-of-town teams. Beck and Roland practiced every few days, and Jet and Kai kept up their strategy of making them believe they'd have an easy victory. They were sloppy sailors whenever the *Viking* was nearby.

But it hadn't been all training. Kai wandered down to the skate park in the afternoons to hang out with the guys, sometimes on his own and sometimes with Oliver tagging along. He missed Tomo and Hiroshi and the rest, but once he got the hang of skateboarding, it was easy to find things to talk about with his new friends.

On Saturdays Kai and Aunt Karin went to the farmers' market. They made a game of trying one of every vegetable they'd never seen before. Kai was amazed to find that carrots came in purple and white and yellow. Aunt Karin became a fan of daikon radishes. And nobody stared at Kai as he and his aunt shopped together. There were plenty of faces as brown as his, and Korean and Spanish were spoken freely

in the market. Jet's friend Skye was half Asian, and nobody seemed to think twice about it.

Jet came downstairs to eat just as Kai was putting the finishing touches on his miso soup. There was a stack of pancakes to rival the Eiffel Tower on the kitchen counter. Uncle Per and Oliver were doing their best to make a dent in the stack. Jet pulled up a plate, but she barely nibbled. She'd been suspicious of Kai's soups in the past, so he didn't bother to ask. He filled a bowl for her and let the steam do its own persuading.

Oliver was nervous, too. He had a thousand worried questions. Kai told Oliver what a careful sailor Jet was, though it wasn't completely true. She sometimes cut a turn a little too close for comfort, and to her mind, there was no point in sailing at all unless you were going to go as fast as possible.

"The main thing," Uncle Per barged in, "is to be good citizens of the river. Yield when you should, even if it costs you your lead."

He got up, took the car keys off the hook, and went outside. Jet watched him go, her eyes lingering on the door. Kai had noticed a circle of worn paint over the kitchen door on his very first night. Every time Uncle Per left the house to pilot a ship over the bar, he reached up and touched his palm to that spot over the door. He'd never said why. Kai had never asked, but the yellow paint was completely gone, leaving a ring of the green the kitchen used to be painted and a hand-size circle of thin white paint over a solid-oak board like a wash of spilled milk. Jet pushed her empty bowl aside and stood up to go. Kai saw her put a bit of Uncle Per's swagger in her walk. Even so, the pilot's mark was out of her reach. She gathered herself for a jump at the door. Her fingers just brushed the edge of the circle.

Kai smiled as he finished off his soup. Jet was the smallest of her friends. Skye towered over her. Bridgie sometimes picked her up off the ground just because she could. If you didn't know Jet, it would be easy to think she was still a little kid, but she worked harder than anyone Kai had ever met, and she cultivated fierceness. Standing on top of her ambitions, that girl was ten feet tall.

At the marina it was the warmest day of the summer so far. A steady wind blew down the river, putting whitecaps on the swells. It would be a rough sail but a fast one. They and the five other teams met with the admiral of the regatta to review the rules and get the

GPS coordinates for the first treasure. It was a timed race. Boats were started twenty minutes apart; the fastest time at the finish won.

The *Saga* won the draw for first choice of start times. Jet had spent all day yesterday calculating travel times. She didn't hesitate. First start would give them the most favorable tide, so long as they could complete the upstream leg of the race in under an hour. Uncle Per went through the checklist, making sure they had all their safety equipment, testing the rescue beacons, and making sure the life jackets fit snugly. Then he reached in his pocket and took out two small slips of paper.

"This is from Karin," he said with a smile.

"Wow!" Jet said. "For us? Look, Kai, it's a rub-on tattoo. Mom makes them for Comic Con."

The design was the outline of the *Saga* and the flags of America and Japan. They put them on their arms below the sleeve of the shorty wet suits Dad had insisted they wear. Even though it was the end of July, the Columbia was punishingly cold.

"I've got something, too," Kai said after Uncle Per walked away. "My grandmother used to make these for me on exam day."

He reached in the pocket of his windbreaker and pulled out two long strips of white cloth. There were kanji drawn in the middle.

"It's a custom. Some people say it's silly, just a good-luck charm, but I think it helps." He held one out to Jet. "You can carry it in your pocket if you want, or you can wear it like this."

He tied the strip of cloth around his head with the kanji over his forehead and his hair all tucked in so it wouldn't blow in his face. It was cool and soft and familiar, and Kai felt a wave of calm pass through his body. He was ready for whatever would come.

"What does it say?" Jet said.

"Usually it says *konjoyō—determination* or something like that."

Jet looked at her headband. Kai turned it so it was right-side up.

"Hey! I've seen these characters before. You wrote that on the geocache log on Saddle Mountain. Is it . . ." Jet looked over his shoulder. The other competitors were all close by. "Isn't this the name of your town?" she whispered.

Kai didn't have to answer. She knew.

"I'd be honored," Jet said quietly.

32

"READY?" JET SAID. A shiver passed through her. This was it, the first step. After all their practices Jet was a hundred percent confident of their chances. Her cousin was the perfect racing partner. All they needed was a little bit of luck and a fair wind. The starter's pistol echoed over the river as Jet pushed off from the dock to the cheers of the crowd. Kai rowed them into the channel, and Jet raised the sails.

They started with a headwind in the wide spot between Mott Island and the Oregon bank of the Columbia. They'd get at least two good tacks in before they'd have to deal with the current from the John Day River.

"Ship oars!" Jet called.

Kai pulled in the oars and moved to the bow while

Jet trimmed the mainsail. Instantly the sail swelled with wind and rocked the *Saga* to the port side. Jet ran as close-hauled as she could. There was the wonderful gurgling noise a sailboat makes when it gets under way. Bubbles streamed out from the rudder, and a wake formed a V of ripples behind them.

Kai took out the GPS and fed in the coordinates of the first treasure. They checked the chart they'd taped to the thwart.

"Looks like the treasure is between Lois Island and Settler Point," Jet said.

"In all those weeds?" Kai asked.

"We'll find it," Jet said, all confidence.

The eastern side of Lois Island was a marsh. Birds loved to nest in the tall grass, but it would be easy to sail right past a hidden cache. Jet headed toward the mouth of the John Day River. It hadn't rained in weeks, and the snow had already melted off the coast range, so the John Day wasn't very full.

"What time is it?" she asked.

"Ten thirty-eight."

They would have another forty minutes of rising tide and then about fifteen of slack current. Luck was with them.

"Excellent!" Jet beamed. "The tide will push the current of the John Day upriver and help move us along even faster."

She got ready for another tack just as they were reaching the mouth of the John Day. Jet squinted at the surface of the river for some hint of where the fresh water was moving.

"There it is," Kai called out, pointing to a stretch of water a dozen yards off the port bow.

"Where?"

"Sediment," Kai said.

There was a swath of brownish water coming out of the river's mouth. The incoming tide pushed the river water up the Columbia before it got lost in the current of the larger river. Jet swung the tiller to move the *Saga* into position.

"Almost there . . . almost there . . . Helms alee!" she called, swinging the tiller as they hit the river current. The *Saga* leapt to the right, and Kai scrambled to get the sails properly trimmed.

"Yes!" Kai hollered as they felt the extra push of the John Day's current moving them along.

"Watch for snags!" Jet called out. "There's usually a bunch in here."

The south channel was a tricky one, twenty-five feet deep in some places and only three in others.

"How's our course?" Jet asked.

"Two miles straight ahead."

They settled into a rhythm of tacking every few minutes, working their way upstream. They slowed quite a bit once the current from the John Day got absorbed into the much larger flow of the Columbia. It was the last push they'd get until they turned down-river. They sailed on between the rocky shore on the south side of the channel and the reeds and weeds on the north side.

"About three hundred feet," Kai said at last. "Can you pull us in tight to the island?"

Jet loosened the mainsheet to pull them alongside the waving reeds and grasses of Lois Island. Kai stood up beside the mast to search.

"See anything?" Jet called.

"Nothing."

"Are we close?"

Kai checked the GPS. "According to this, we're sixty feet from it. It's got to be right here!"

"There's no such thing as a perfect signal," Jet said. "Keep looking. It's bright red. How hard can it be?"

"We're past it," Kai said a minute later. He turned the GPS unit so Jet could read the distance counter. It was at ninety feet and rising. "Can you turn us around?"

Jet sucked in a breath. This was the narrowest spot in the channel. The railroad tracks on the Oregon bank were less than a stone's throw away.

"It'll have to be a quick one," Jet said.

She looked over her shoulder to calculate the distance and the strength of the wind.

"There it is!" she hollered.

Across the channel a railroad trestle bridged the small cove in front of Settler Point. Halfway up the trestle was a red box.

"Treasure, ho!" Jet called.

They swung the boat around and brought it alongside the bridge. A brand-new cleat to tie up boats had been screwed into the bridge support. A line of steel spikes like they put on telephone poles went up to the crossbeam where the box rested.

Kai took the tiller, and Jet scrambled up. She flipped open the latch of the treasure box. Inside were a dozen bronze-colored coins that had been stamped with a sailboat and the points of a compass. On the

reverse it said TREASURE ISLAND RACE. Inside the lid was a note.

"Well done, Hawkins!" it said in curling piratical script. "Your voyage is one-third complete. Here are the coordinates for Flint's chest of silver doubloons."

There was a number and a grease pencil. Jet hastily copied it on her arm and hustled down to the boat. A long smear of tar got on the front of her life jacket, and the smell of creosote was pungent on her hands, but she barely noticed as they pushed off for the next leg of the race.

Jet checked over her shoulder for the red mast of the *Viking*. Beck and Roland had drawn second start and would be right behind them. Their boat was at the mouth of the John Day. She hoped they hadn't seen her climbing the trestle. She'd been sorely tempted to cheat and make the treasure box just a little bit harder to find.

Kai put the new coordinates in their GPS. Jet steered them around Settler Point, toward Russian Island.

"Where are we headed?" Jet called out.

"Take a look," Kai said, showing her the GPS unit. Its red arrow pointed the way.

"How is our tide holding?" Jet asked.

"We'll make it if we keep to our pace," Kai said.

Jet glanced at the chart. "Looks like our next treasure is past Russian Island and past Karlson Island, too."

"I think it's going to be in the middle of Marsh Island," Kai said, leaning back to look at the map upside down.

"Lots of channels in there," Jet said.

"So which side of the island has the strongest current?" Kai asked.

"North." Jet swung the tiller and trimmed the sail closer to the wind. "We should use it while we've got it."

"The ship channel's on that side," Kai said.

"It's race day! Now or never."

"I'm with you," Kai said. "Just saying, there could be some really big ships."

"If we don't push every advantage, Beck and Roland are going to blow right past us," Jet said.

In spite of Kai's predictions, the boys had practiced in the last month. Not as much as Jet and Kai, but Beck had always been a good sailor, and Roland, annoying as he was, learned pretty quickly. Jet felt a knot grow in her stomach. Uncle Lars had emailed

her three weeks ago, back when things at the power plant had been at their worst. It was a short message thanking her for asking Kai to sail in the race. Saying that in the worst and longest days, it gave him peace of mind to know Kai was out there on his home river having the time of his life. No way was she going to let her uncle down.

Kai had come so far since their first sails together a month ago. He was an able sailor from the start and understood instinctively how to handle a boat like the *Saga,* but he'd spent those early sails fighting down panic, especially on the foggy mornings. He was rock steady now, but Jet had come to understand that her cousin was always going to be a more cautious sailor than her. Something Dad heartily approved of.

"I'll keep plenty of room between us and the ship channel," Jet said.

They passed a race official's boat and the coast guard lifeboat. The official waved the *Saga* on. Jet couldn't resist checking on the *Viking.* It was steadily closing the gap. They were so close she could hear Beck and Roland arguing.

"It's not over yet," Kai said firmly.

When they turned into the channel between Snag

Island and Marsh Island, Jet lost sight of the *Viking*. Kai started counting down the distance on the GPS unit.

Jet backed off the wind, slowing the boat and swinging closer to the north shore. There were a few overgrown channels, but none big enough for a sailboat.

"There!" Kai shouted a moment later, pointing to the mouth of a channel wider than the others and with no overhanging trees.

"Helms alee!" Jet moved the tiller hard to the right. The *Saga* nosed into the channel and lost the wind completely. It was like sailing into a closet. Not a breath.

"Now what are we going to do?" Kai said.

"Can you see the bottom?" Jet asked.

"Nope."

The channel was edged around with reeds. It thrummed with frog noises. Jet stuck an oar straight down in the still water. When it hit mud she drew the oar out and stood to measure it against her body. The water was up to her neck.

"I don't think we can hop out and tow it," Jet said.

Actually they probably could. Kai was tall enough, but she couldn't bring herself to ask him to walk along a channel bottom they couldn't see, in waters that were clearly piled with frog poop. Not when he'd refused to swim or even go wading all summer long. He'd only just gotten brave enough to look for submerged snags in the water.

"I'll row," Kai said. "You steer."

Jet slipped her oar back in the lock, and Kai sat on the thwart to row. She stood up at the tiller to better spot the treasure. The GPS numbers clicked lower and lower as they followed the channel's winding turns.

"Know what's great about this?" Jet said. "We're the only boat small enough to have oars. Everyone else has canoe paddles instead. We're going to be way faster than any of those longer boats in this tiny channel."

"Should be right around here," Kai said, glancing at the GPS.

"Look." Jet pointed to an oversize nest tucked in among the branches. A few bits of blue-green eggshell rested inside. A pure-white shorebird stalked out of the tall grass, looked at the boat, and then lifted off with an impossibly slow wing beat. Two baby birds followed. Jet stopped and took a breath. Gray herons were all over the place, but these white ones were rare; it felt lucky to see them take to the sky.

"There!" Kai shouted.

The second treasure box was in the V of some willow branches. This time they didn't have to climb for it. The chest held silver coins and the coordinates for the third treasure. By the time they rowed out of the channel and back into the river, the tide was completely slack, and the river current was pushing them backward. Jet swung the nose of the *Saga* around to start the third leg of the race. She glanced over her shoulder, and there was the *Viking,* closing the gap. Jet swore like a sea captain.

"Gambare!" Kai said. "It's not over yet."

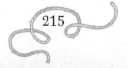

33

"THE WIND IS still in our favor," Kai said. "If we take longer tacks, we'll pull ahead."

He was sure of it. If they tacked more efficiently like they'd practiced, if they took longer before each turn, then logically they should win.

But now the *Viking* was closing the gap again, and Kai felt doubts creep in. Everyone at the power plant was rooting for him. They'd finally turned the corner on their problems at the end of last week. Today was the first day off they'd had in more than a month. The thought of disappointing them made Kai physically sick. But the white cranes they'd seen when they found the second treasure—they were good luck. Obāsan had always said so, especially a mother and baby cranes. Their luck would turn. He could feel it.

"We've got to find the next treasure quick," Jet said. "Or we'll be fighting the outgoing tide along with the river's current."

The day was heating up. Kai passed Jet a water bottle. A few spectators in boats cheered them on as they rounded Quinns Island, and then they had one last island to pass before they turned downriver and headed for the finish line.

"Looks like the third treasure is on the other side of Tenasillahe," Jet said. "Good thing. The sooner we turn toward the ocean, the better."

Jet and Kai passed another race officials' boat. They marked the *Saga*'s time and waved them along the course.

"Okay, ready for the turnaround?" Jet called. The ship channel passed through the narrow spot between Tenasillahe and Puget Islands. Jet looked upriver and saw the way clear. But downriver there was a container ship just clearing the passage between the two islands.

"Whoa!" Kai said. "How will we get past that?"

"Don't worry about it," Jet said, "By the time we catch up to it, it'll be in a wider spot in the river."

When they made the turn around the east end of the island and back toward the ocean, Kai could feel

the pull the current gave them. It was like a magnet. Even Jet was surprised at how strong it was.

"Yeah!" she yelled, letting the mainsail all the way out over the port rail to let the *Saga* run before the wind.

Kai pulled the jib sail to starboard so they were sailing wing on wing for maximum speed.

"Yatta!" he shouted, laughing as they sped along faster than they'd ever gone before. Their luck was turning. He knew it. The tide was going out now, and the *Viking* would have to make the last upstream bit of the race fighting both the current and the tide. Kai felt confidence pouring in. He'd make his father proud. He'd make them all proud.

"How far to the next treasure?" Jet called.

"About half a mile," Kai said.

They had deep water and plenty of room. They let the *Saga* run. In no time they gained on the container ship, which was slowing to make a turn. Just off the starboard side was a sailboat about the same size as the *Saga*.

"Wait! Who's that?" Jet called. "Did somebody pass us?"

"No," Kai said. "Look. She's got a blue dolphin on

her sail. There's no *Blue Dolphin* in the race. Beck and Roland are the only ones close enough to pass us."

They both looked upriver in time to see the *Viking* make the turn around Tenasillahe Island.

"How did they catch up to us so fast?" Jet shouted, a note of panic in her voice.

They'd been counting on the tide to slow Beck and Roland down on the upstream side of the race. It was the only hope they had. Already the catamaran was feeling the benefit of the river current.

"Not over yet," Kai said, looking at Jet with complete confidence.

"The current would be faster in deeper water," she said.

She swung the tiller toward the shipping channel. They sailed on, Jet with one eye on the container ship ahead and one eye on the *Viking* closing the gap.

"Wake!" Kai hollered as the whitecapped V that came off the stern of the ship rocked the *Saga* side to side. He was leaning forward, searching the way ahead for any scrap of advantage he could find.

Jet gripped the rail and held the tiller steady. Kai threw a glance over his shoulder. The *Viking* would be a lot more vulnerable to rough water, with the way

it was riding up on one hull in the wind. Would they risk the faster water closer to the ship channel or play it safe in shallower water? Beck was too good a sailor to take a chance he didn't need to, and it was his boat. But Roland had the stronger personality and a reckless streak. Kai could hear him arguing with Beck.

It was a foolish mistake to contend with a captain. Kai would never second-guess his cousin, if only because the confidence she gained from his support made her a better sailor every day. He'd been happy to hear the bickering aboard the *Viking* at the start of the race, when it had looked like it would work to the *Saga*'s advantage. But now that he thought about the danger of jockeying for leadership in the middle of the race with high winds and a strong current, Kai felt sick at heart.

He scanned the river for other boats. The race officials were on the far side of Tenasillahe Island, and he hadn't seen the coast guard since clear back at the Jim Crow Sands. Where was everybody? No, he shook off his doubts. Beck knew the river, and he loved the *Viking* too much to risk losing her.

The wind blew so strong it sang in the stays and halyards of the *Saga,* but there was no competing with

the lighter catamaran. It flew past Jet and Kai, riding high on one hull. Roland let out a victory whoop, and Kai could hear Beck laughing as they angled in front of the *Saga,* leaving Jet and Kai to eat wake.

"Gambare," Kai said grimly.

34

"WE'RE DOOMED," JET said. "We can't out-run them in this." She hung her head and let the *Saga* drift a bit closer to the ship channel than she should.

"We can outthink them in this," Kai said sharply. "Come on, Jet. You know this river. Where's that treasure?"

Kai watched Jet call up a mental picture of the ship channel that she'd drawn out by hand every day for the last month.

"Welch Island is too swampy," she said, looking up. "A treasure box there would sink. Tenasillahe has sand. But there are piles, see?" She pointed to the shore of the nearest river island. "They're submerged now, but we saw them last week when the tide was lower. Right below the osprey nest. Remember? They wouldn't put the treasure there, either—too danger-ous. It'll be on the beach right before Red Slough." She pointed to a level stretch of sand.

"Are you sure?" Kai said.

They both watched the *Viking* speed past the spot without changing course. Beck and Roland were busy managing the sail. Neither boy was looking at the GPS.

"Solid," Jet said.

She swung the tiller to bring them in. Kai leaned out over the bow, searching the beach. The *Viking* sped ahead, but Kai trusted his cousin's call. The new boat fed Beck's confidence more than it should. He and Roland were laughing when they should be sailing. Kai remembered his lucky cranes and searched.

"Treasure!" he shouted, a few minutes later. He banged his palms on the deck like it was a *taiko* drum. "We've got them now!"

Kai pointed the way, and Jet set a course by his guidance. Kai's heart was hammering. He knew a way to cut their time on the turnaround, but it would mean he'd have to do the one thing he'd been avoiding the entire summer. In all their sails he'd never actually set foot in the water. He'd wanted to, but something about the way mists gathered over the water every morning

made him hesitate. Obā-san had loved ghost stories. And in all her stories, that space where water and sky met was haunted. He didn't believe in ghosts, not really. But somewhere thousands of miles away, somewhere in this same ocean, his grandparents were lost. It would be like stepping into their graves.

And yet the treasure was so close! They had this one chance to take the championship. To win it in his father's boat. He could feel his whole town watching from home. Yes. He had to try, no matter what it cost him in nightmares.

"Jet!" Kai shouted. "Don't run her aground. Just bring her in close, and turn her nose back out. I don't want to lose one second beaching and then shoving off." Kai crouched in the bow of the boat, eyeing the distance to shore.

"Kai, wait!"

"It's okay. I want to."

"But—" Jet looked torn. She would sacrifice the time for him if he asked. She was that kind of a captain.

"It's cold," Jet said. "Really cold. Don't let it shock you."

Kai handed her the jib sheet. "Trust me."

"Ten more yards, and you'll be in three feet of water," she said.

She held the course steady.

"I can see the bottom," Kai shouted.

"Now!" Jet yelled.

Kai jumped. Time froze for a moment as he leapt over the water. The grief he'd pushed away all summer long came roaring out of him like fire. He let out a yell that burned his throat. Jet pulled in the tiller and hauled in the mainsheet to make the turn. Kai thrashed out of the water, freezing even in his wetsuit. He threw open the chest, grabbed a gold token, and ran back to the water just as wind filled the *Saga*'s sails.

"Come on!" Jet yelled.

Kai popped the treasure in his mouth, ran into the water until he was waist deep, and then dove for the stern of the *Saga*. He closed the distance in a few strokes. He spit the treasure out into the bottom of the sailboat. It rocked dangerously to one side as Kai hauled himself aboard.

"Got it!" he gasped.

Water rolled off of him. And grief and fear.

"You did it!" Jet shouted. She grabbed Kai by the shoulder of his life jacket and pulled him up. "We're going to win this thing. Look!"

The *Viking* was still charging ahead. Now they'd have to fight the wind and the current to get back upstream to the third treasure.

Kai shook water from his hair. He moved to his post, took the jib sheet, and waited for his captain's command. He could feel it. Wind, current, tide, luck—it was all running in their favor.

A moment later they heard shouting aboard the *Viking.*

"I think they finally checked their GPS," Jet said, grinning like mad. "They've got a fight on their hands now."

She didn't take her eyes from their course for a second. They were coming to a narrower spot in the river, and the container ship, the *Viking,* and that spectator in the *Blue Dolphin* would have little room to maneuver. Kai was already anticipating the tack the *Viking* would have to make. He worked out the right-of-way in his head. The rules for how you could pass another sailboat were tricky, and they shifted according to the

wind. There was more shouting aboard the *Viking,* and then they took a completely different turn.

"What the heck!" Jet hollered. "They can't do that! It's against the—"

"No!" Kai groaned.

They took a wrong tack. Cut off the *Blue Dolphin*'s right-of-way. They were on a collision course with the smaller boat. Both boys were looking at the GPS, and nobody was steering.

"Look out!" Jet yelled at triple her usual volume.

Fear gripped Kai so he couldn't speak. Any luck he'd wished for himself he now wished for the *Viking* and the *Blue Dolphin,* which was about to get run over. The smaller boat made an abrupt swerve. There was a shriek of terror and the sound of a splash.

"What was that?" Jet shouted.

Kai searched the waters ahead. The *Viking* had finished its turn and was heading upriver toward the third treasure, but the *Blue Dolphin*'s mainsheet was dragging in the water on the starboard side. There was no one at the tiller.

"Man overboard!" he yelled.

35

"Let's go!" Kai shouted. "We could save him!"

Without a thought for the race, Jet swerved from the course and headed for the drowning man.

"Do you see him?" she called.

Kai stood up, a hand on the mast.

"I don't."

"He's got to be there somewhere. The other side of the boat?"

Kai put a foot on each rail to gain some height. He searched for the ring of ripples that would show where the man went in.

"Come on, where are you?" Jet said to the water. "Nobody just sinks without a fight."

"Just get us there," Kai said. "We'll find him."

Jet closed in on the unmanned *Blue Dolphin*. It was

moving in a slow arc that would take it right in the path of the container ship. Jet heard shouting from the *Viking* and then a splash. The catamaran turned, and the wind dumped out of its sails. Jet could see Roland at the tiller. Beck was nowhere in sight.

"Beck!" Jet hollered.

She stood up to look for him; the tiller slipped out of her hand. The *Saga* lurched to one side and lost the wind.

"Steady," Kai called. "He's right there."

The empty *Blue Dolphin* continued on its collision course with the container ship, but now Jet could see a bearded man thrashing in the river and Beck swimming toward him. Beck was a strong swimmer, but the drowning man would pull him under in a heartbeat.

"No!" Jet yelled.

She looked upriver for the coast guard. Their lifeboat was at the far end of the island, facing the other way. The whistle on her life jacket would never be heard over the container ship's engines. Jet lit her rescue beacon and clipped it to a life ring. The beacon would ping every coast guard radar for miles. It was Beck's and the drowning man's only chance.

"Kai! Take this and throw it when we get close!"

Kai grabbed the makeshift life ring and pointed the course for Jet to keep.

"Can't that ship see we're in trouble down here?" Kai said. "They're not stopping."

"Not a chance," Jet said. "We're in the ship's blind spot. Besides, it takes them a mile to stop. And they'll run aground if they go out of the shipping lane. Don't worry, I'll be careful."

Jet gripped the tiller harder. She wasn't being careful, and she knew it. The wind was fluky in the shadow of the ship, and the water was rough between the bow and stern wakes.

"Almost there," Kai shouted.

He pointed the way. Jet squinted against the spray and saw nothing but trusted her cousin's eye. The drowning man's head bobbed with the swells. He thrashed his arms to keep afloat, and Beck drew steadily closer.

"Come on, Coasties, where are you?" Jet said under her breath.

The rescue beacon was flashing its red light. At least Beck and the man overboard were out of the path of the container ship. Jet and Kai had nearly closed the gap when they heard another scream. At first Jet

thought it might be a bird, but then it came again, the unmistakable shrill voice of a child.

"Daaaaaddy!"

"Oh no, there's a kid!" Jet shouted. "Where is he?" She scanned the water.

Kai was still standing on the rails in front of the mast. "I don't see him."

"Check the boat. Is he still in there?" Jet said, fighting to keep the *Saga* on a steady course.

"There!" Kai shouted. A little kid cowered in the bottom of the *Blue Dolphin,* hands gripping the rail, his head just showing over the side.

"Toss that life ring," Jet yelled. "Beck can handle it. We've got to get that kid!"

Jet steeled herself to turn the *Saga* away from the drowning man and straight into the path of the container ship. Her courage plummeted to her toes. What if . . . What if . . . No, she told herself, gripping the tiller. Stay the course. Beck's a strong swimmer. The coast guard's on the way. If someone was going to catch that kid before 70,000 tons of steel ran him over, it would have to be her and Kai.

"Ready about!" she called.

Kai heaved the life ring toward the Beck and the

drowning man. Kai hopped off the rails and manned the jib sheet. Once they'd turned in the direction of the rogue sailboat, Kai took the spare boat cushion and some rope and made another life ring.

Jet held the tiller steady as the *Saga* hit the bow wake of the container ship. They were nearly even with the front of the ship now. She could hear shouting from the deck, and a moment later the engine noises shifted to a lower drone.

"They've seen us!" Kai shouted. "They're stopping."

"They'll never stop in time!" Jet said. She squinted in the sunlight as they came out of the shadow of the ship. The *Blue Dolphin* made a sweeping arc across the river. Jet picked a spot to head it off. She looked back to check on Beck. He was a few feet from the drowning man, pushing the life ring toward him.

"But if the captain up there buys us a few minutes . . ." She looked back at the bow of the ship. It towered four stories above them. "Or a bit of sailing room."

"Just get me close enough to throw a rope," Kai said, steady as a rock.

"I'll get you there."

The wind picked up once they were out of the lee of the ship.

"Hold on!" Kai called out to the kid in the *Blue Dolphin.*

Jet looked over her shoulder and saw the coast guard lifeboat heading toward Beck at top speed. She heaved a sigh of relief. They gained on the *Blue Dolphin,* close enough to hear the kid inside whimpering.

"Hold her steady!" Kai called.

Jet turned a few points north to give Kai a better angle and let the wind spill out of the sails. He heaved the boat cushion. It fell short by a few feet.

"Try again," Jet said.

The container ship came closer. She could see the steel claw of the port-side bow anchor. There was a Moroccan flag and the name GLOBAL PROSPERITY painted on the hull. Jet held steady while Kai tried again. This time the cushion landed in the boat. Kai drew the *Blue Dolphin* alongside the *Saga.*

"Hey!" he called to the kid. "Are you okay?"

The boy was kindergarten size. He held the rail with a death grip. Jet gave the tiller a quick look. It was a sailboat's most vulnerable piece, and it seemed to be in place.

"Can you sail her alone?" Jet said.

"I won't be alone," Kai said. "I've got good crew. I

can tell." He smiled at the boy. "Ready to go get your dad? He's right there." Kai pointed across the river. "We're all going to make it home."

"Hurry," Jet muttered quietly. The *Global Prosperity* was so close, she could smell the rusted iron of her hull.

"Hang on," Kai said. "She's going to rock when I come aboard."

The boy scooted to the mast and wrapped his arms around it. Kai boarded the *Blue Dolphin* and sat at the tiller.

"Go, Kai!" Jet said. "Go!" She pushed them off. Kai pulled in the mainsail and swerved out of the path of the container ship.

Jet scrambled to pull her mainsail over to the port side to catch the wind, but Kai had moved the jib to starboard to get more room to throw the line. Jet opened the tiller extension so she could inch forward to reach the jib sheet and bring the front sail under control.

The shadow of the *Global Prosperity* fell over her boat. A shiver rose up her spine. She held the mainsheet in her teeth and snagged the jib sheet with her

free hand. She gave the rope a tug to pull the jib sail to the port side, but it was too late.

The container ship passed her, cutting off the wind. A second later the bow wake rocked the *Saga* violently and tore the tiller extension from her hand. The boat spun in a tight circle, and by the time Jet had dodged the swinging boom and slid back to the stern to regain the tiller, the sail was flapping wildly and blocking her view. When the *Saga* struck the side of the container ship a moment later, it made a tiny ping against the vast metal surface, but the force of it was enough to throw Jet forward and strike her head against the thwart.

"No!" she groaned, pushing herself back into place. She took the tiller, but with no wind there was no way to steer. Worse was the grinding sound of fiberglass against steel. The *Saga*'s patched hull broke. A split opened up that went the length of the boat. Jet heard it, felt it, like a knife through her own skin. Gurgling water filled the buoyancy space along the starboard side. The *Saga* dipped toward the ship; the top of the mast clanged against its side.

Jet could hear voices calling from the deck far

above but couldn't make out the words. The *Saga* no longer answered her tiller. Water was coming out of the hold covers and filling the space where Jet stood. Someone lowered a bright yellow rope from the deck of the *Global Prosperity,* but it was beyond her reach. The thrum of the ship's propellers grew louder as she came closer to the stern.

Jet had seen ship propellers at the Maritime Museum. They were as tall as her house. The waters of the Columbia rose dark and cold in her boat. Could she swim for it? The coast guard wasn't far, but she didn't have her rescue beacon anymore. Would they see her? Hear her over the sound of the ship? Was she strong enough to swim clear of the propellers? Jet had never felt less strong in her life. She was amidships now, and she knew the sooner she abandoned the *Saga,* the better chance she had.

And then she saw the pilot's ladder, right where it should be. Jet checked the straps on her life jacket. Took one last glance at her boat. Water came over the starboard rail. She kept an eye on the pilot's ladder. It was about four feet above the waterline. She'd never reach it if she fell in the water. She'd only have one

jump. The top of the mast scraped along the side of the container ship, leaving a line on its peeling paint.

"Almost there . . . ," Jet coached herself.

She'd seen videos of bar pilots making the jump. A pilot boat was huge compared to the *Saga*. There was a spot on the deck where the pilot stood to wait for the ladder to come in reach. It had special nonskid deck coating and a break in the rail to make it easier. No such luck for her. Jet gripped the port rail, ready to spring. There was a chatter of voices above her. The yellow rope was almost in reach.

Jet took one deep breath, gritted her teeth. She stepped from the port rail to the boom, swung her arms forward, and jumped with all her strength. Her hands found the sides of the ladder a fraction of a second before her chin slammed into the side of the ship. Her feet missed completely. She was dangling by her arms.

Her head throbbed from the bruising. She pulled her knees up and then pressed the soles of her sneakers against the side of the ship. She walked up the side, inching her hands upward until she could get her feet on the lowest rung of the ladder. The yellow rope was

right beside her now. Jet looked upward, squinting, to see two faces leaning over the side, calling to her in a language she didn't understand.

The *Saga* slid toward the stern of the ship, riding lower in the water every second. Jet watched, mesmerized, as the stern wake pushed it away from the *Global Prosperity*. Her boat drifted a hundred yards, heeled over, and sank.

36

KAI SPENT HIS first heart-stopping seconds aboard the *Blue Dolphin* turning it away from the path of the container ship, away from the bar with its treacherous currents, away from the bitter-cold ocean. He spent the next few seconds trimming the sails. As he scrambled for the new course, he checked off the boat's working parts. Tiller and mainsheet first—because without them he couldn't steer—and then the other systems one by one.

The *Blue Dolphin* was newer than the *Saga,* but she wasn't as well kept. Rust in the pulleys made it slow work to turn her sails. On the first tack Kai found the problem. The hiking strap that held the boom at the bottom of the sail in place had broken, probably when the *Viking* cut them off and they had to make an abrupt turn. The strap was frayed at the edges to begin with, and the stress of the sudden swerve had snapped it.

There was nothing on hand to fix it. And even if there was, Kai needed both hands to sail the boat. He tried to coax the boy out of his curled-up position in the bow so he could hold the tiller steady while Kai fixed the boom. But the kid wouldn't budge. Wouldn't talk. Wouldn't even look at Kai.

Kai promised the boy that his father was safe. Showed him where the coast guard was speeding away with his father on board. Promised that they'd be right behind them.

No response.

Kai sighed and turned his attention to the boat. They could sail with the broken strap, but it would take all his concentration. He trimmed the sails as best he could and headed for the finish line.

Once he got the hang of the new boat, they picked up a little speed, but every time Kai took a tack and the boom swung across the deck, the boy screamed in terror. The sound of it pierced Kai's heart. He knew the boy was remembering how his dad had been swept overboard—seeing it happen again in that mental

movie you get that's more vivid than life and impossible to look away from. The boy was crouched with his arms wrapped around his knees, shivering.

The Red Cross woman who'd helped Kai at the airport when he was leaving Japan had said, "You're going to be okay. You'll be safe now." At the time the words didn't reach him, and he'd sat frozen with fear the whole plane ride from Osaka. Some things couldn't be fixed with words. Kai could only bring the boy home.

They finally reached the finish line, long after the other boats in the race had zipped ahead. The coast guard was standing by. Beck and the boy's father were waiting for them. Both of them were wrapped in warming blankets and were hovered over by a medic. When the boat touched the dock, the boy leapt into his father's arms. Cameras flashed all around. The breath Kai didn't realize he'd been holding whooshed out of him. His hands started to shake. They'd come so close to that container ship. He'd heard the thrum of its engines, felt the vibration of them on his skin, smelled the tang of rusted steel. A few minutes longer, and they would have been lost.

No. He wouldn't think about that. He'd done the correct thing, and the boy had lived.

And he'd lost the race, he realized, seeing all the other crews congratulate the winning boat. He tied up the *Blue Dolphin* and made his way toward the winners to do the same. Halfway there a man in a coast guard uniform stopped him.

"Hey there! Crew of the *Saga!*" he boomed, extending a hand.

"Hello," Kai said, shaking the man's hand. "I'm Kai. Kai Ellstrom."

"I know who you are," the man said, continuing to pump Kai's arm. "That was some incredible sailing back there. Grace under pressure. You are the man!"

"Oh, um . . . yes," Kai said, a little flustered. "You pulled Beck and the man out of the river. That was amazing. Thank you!"

The Coastie smiled and thumped Kai on the back. "I train to do this stuff full time. You're the amazing one. Listen—ordinarily my crew and I would buy you a drink."

Kai blushed furiously.

"How about you come by the station tomorrow and tell us your story?"

He turned Kai around to look at the rescued man

talking to reporters. The boy was clinging to his father like he'd never let go.

"That sight just never gets old," he said. "You're a lifesaver now, Ellstrom. You'll always be one of us." The coast guardsman thumped him on the back one more time and then walked away.

"Bring that cousin of yours along tomorrow," he called over his shoulder. "Looks like she's got a story to tell, too."

Jet! The *Saga*! Kai had been so focused on saving the kid, he'd forgotten them. He looked back over the racecourse, confident that Jet would be right behind him.

The river was empty of sails.

37

JET LOCKED HER left arm around the rail of the pilot's ladder. The river licked at her feet. She grabbed the yellow rope and threaded it through the straps of her life jacket. Using her right hand and her teeth, she made an anchor hitch to secure herself to the lifeline and then worked her way up. It had never been hard to climb the ladder when she was practicing in the barn, but with wet hands and muscles already tired from hours of sailing, her feet slipped, and every motion felt weighed down. Her dad had once described it as running up three flights of fire escape with an outside chance of drowning. It had sounded funny at the time, but now Jet felt every inch of the climb in her hands and shoulders and aching legs.

"One more step," Jet told herself again and again.

Resting a dozen rungs from the top, she turned and looked back. The *Saga* was gone. The coast guard lifeboat was stopped at the spot where Beck had saved the drowning man, and Kai and the rescued kid in the *Blue Dolphin* were speeding home, sails set wing on wing.

At the top a half-dozen deckhands helped her over the rail. One of them immediately draped her in a woolen blanket. Another untied the lifeline. They were grizzled and wrinkly and missing a few teeth, but Jet had never been happier to see anyone in her life. They spoke to her all at once in what sounded like Arabic. Jet tried out "thank you" in every language she could think of. When she got to *"gracias,"* she was met with approving nods and smiles. She glanced around for an officer. English was the language of international shipping, so there had to be a few people aboard who spoke it.

"Greetings," came a voice from among the deckhands. The men parted, and Jet caught sight of a man only slightly taller than herself but wearing an officer's cap. He was younger than the crew. Jet guessed he would be the second or third mate. He had a medical kit under his arm.

"Are you well?" he asked with a concerned look.

"Yes," Jet said. She put on a smile. Her head ached, her chin was bleeding, and she was freezing cold, but no way was she going to complain.

"Your face is injured," the mate said.

Jet put a hand to her chin and felt her rapidly swelling lip.

He took an ice pack out of the medical kit.

"May I present, Miss?" He pulled a handkerchief from his pocket and wrapped the ice pack in it before handing it over.

Jet took the pack and pressed it to her chin. The sting of cold made her eyes water. I made the jump, she thought. I did it! And immediately a picture of Captain Chandler in his wheelchair filled her mind. She could still hear the thrum of the propeller. She could feel it with her feet. It all could have gone differently.

"You are able to walk a little farther?" the mate went on earnestly. "My captain is eager to meet you."

Jet followed the mate across the deck, past rows of stacked shipping containers, and into the interior of the ship. It was quite a bit farther than Jet thought it would be. She followed him through dim passageways

and up more flights of stairs, but it was worth it when she reached the top.

The bridge was a bright room with windows all around, about the size of her school classroom. Every surface was covered with dials and gauges and data screens. There was a chart table and the wheel in the center.

A black man in a captain's uniform turned away from the chart. "*Salaam alaikum,*" he said. "Welcome aboard, Miss. I am Captain Amrani."

Jet wiped the river water off her hand and held it out. "*Salaam alaikum.* Thank you, Captain."

She glanced at the crew in the room. The helmsman had his hand on the wheel. Another officer sat in front of a radio. The mate who brought her up stood by the door. The river pilot was at the helm. Jet wondered if she could be arrested for not yielding to a container ship. There were rules on the river. Lots of them. Jet stood up straighter.

"Sir, I apologize for striking your ship and for this unauthorized boarding. It was done in the course of a rescue. There was a man overboard and a little child left alone and unable to sail his boat, only a hundred

yards off your port bow. It was all in your blind spot, and there was no one else to help."

The radioman burst in with an urgent comment in Arabic. The river pilot called out the course as they hugged the curve of the Washington shore between Skamokawa and Three Tree Point.

"I have news you will be glad to hear," Captain Amrani said. "Your friend is safe. The man he rescued will recover, and the two children in the sailboat are a hundred meters from shore."

"My cousin," Jet said, beaming. "Kai Ellstrom. He's a brilliant sailor!"

"Ellstrom?" The river pilot said with a smile. "He wouldn't be a relative of Captain Per Ellstrom, now would he?" He directed the helmsman to cross over to the Oregon side of the river.

"Yes, he's—"

"You're Jet Ellstrom, aren't you?" the pilot said without taking his eyes off the river. "I'd know you anywhere."

"You would?" Jet looked at him more closely, wondering if she'd met him before. River pilots spent more time in Portland than in Astoria, but her dad seemed to know every mariner under the sun.

"Blue eyes and bravado. Yeah, you're Captain Ellstrom's girl, all right." He held out his hand. "Captain Gray."

They shook, and then Jet took a look at the chart; the paper copy and an electronic one sat side by side. It was just like the one she'd been studying. She pored over the instruments. The compass was obvious, but there were a dozen unfamiliar displays in front of the pilot.

"Wind speed," he said, tapping a dial in front of him. "Wind direction, radar, engine speed."

Jet drank it in with eager ears. She asked one question after another. The pilot showed her the fathometer, the gyro compass repeater, and the rudder angle indicator. He explained how the engine order telegraph worked, while the captain continued his conversation on the radio. Eventually the captain came and stood beside the river pilot. "So you are learning to navigate?" Captain Armani said.

Jet nodded eagerly. "That's my plan!"

"It's a very long road from where you're standing to where I'm standing," the river pilot said.

"I can climb the ladder. That's a start."

"A fine start," Captain Amrani said, beaming.

"An even better start would be learning to use the helicopter."

"What?"

"Much as we welcome your good company here on the *Global Prosperity,* your parents will wish for your safe return. Although the use of the pilot boat and ladder is customary here in the river, it is my wish that you leave my ship by helicopter. It is safer. The coast guard will retrieve you as part of their rescue operation."

Jet stared at him, her mouth open, hardly daring to believe it. She thought she'd be an old woman before she even got a chance to ride a helicopter. The mate grinned at her like a little kid.

"This will allow your coast guard to demonstrate a rescue procedure in view of the many spectators at your sailing race today." Captain Amrani smiled. "I believe cheering will be involved."

"Oh my gosh!" Jet was breathless. "I would love that—more than anything!"

The river pilot gave the command to turn the *Global Prosperity* at Tongue Point. When they reached Astoria, the pilot boat pulled alongside. The mate scurried off to bring the bar pilot to the bridge so Captain Gray could hand over the command. A woman in the

yellow-and-black jacket of a bar pilot came through the door a few moments later.

"Captain Dempsey!" Jet said.

"Jet Ellstrom, I hear you've had a hell of a race today," Captain Dempsey said.

"Yes, ma'am!"

She greeted Captain Amrani, shook hands with Captain Gray, and then enveloped Jet in a quick hug.

"You know how long I've waited to come aboard and find another woman?"

"Um . . . forever?" Jet said.

"Am I going to see you up on this bridge someday?"

"Working on it."

"Don't listen to her, Jet," Captain Gray said with a smile. "Be a river pilot—all the beauty of the Columbia and a fraction of the danger."

"I think this one has a heart for danger," Captain Amrani said.

"You take all that courage, add some knowledge and experience, and you'll do just fine," Captain Dempsey said.

"Plenty of time to decide," Captain Gray added.

"Now about the helicopter," Captain Dempsey went on. "Are you ready for that?"

Jet bounced on her toes with excitement.

"Listen, if you get scared up there, just look straight up the cable, and do exactly as the surfman tells you. They'll take good care of you."

"Good to know," Jet said, grinning like crazy. She turned to Captain Gray and shook his hand. "Thank you!" she said, pointing to the instruments he'd shown her. "I won't forget."

She turned to Captain Amrani. "Sir, thank you for rescuing me. This was awesome!"

"Blessings on your journey, child," Captain Amrani said.

Jet took one last look around the bridge, promising herself she'd earn her way back there, no matter what it took. She gave Captain Dempsey another quick hug and headed down the stairs with Captain Gray.

A few minutes later Jet stood atop the shipping containers. She could hear the coast guard helicopter almost as soon as it lifted off from Air Station Astoria. It gave Jet goose bumps to see it darting over the river like a big noisy dragonfly. It approached and hovered. The whop-whop of the rotors was so loud it made her teeth rattle, and the wash of air felt like it was going to push her right off the platform. A surfman in orange

coveralls and a white helmet was lowered onto the deck. When his feet touched down, he waved Jet over. The noise and pulse of the air made Jet's heart race.

"Ready for the ride of your life?" the surfman yelled.

He handed her a helmet and pointed up the cable to the helicopter, fifty feet above them. Jet looked up. The helicopter door was open, and she could just see another helmeted head leaning out and looking down the cable.

"Yes!" she shouted. "Yes!" She jumped and threw her hands in the air.

The surfman laughed and snapped her into the harness and helmet. "Ready?"

Jet grabbed hold of the cable and nodded. The yard or two of slack cable that was lying on the deck beside them rose up, and then with a breathtaking lurch, Jet and the surfman lifted off. They spun in circles like bait on a hook, and Jet waved wildly to the crew on the bridge.

The sunlight on the Columbia Bar made the water sparkle as if it were strewn with diamonds. The water was darker blue and smoother in the channels on either side of the bar. From directly above she could see that the bar was like a mountain of sand blocking the

path up the river. She'd traced the chart a dozen times already. But seeing the real thing, seeing how small the *Global Prosperity* looked beside it, a thousand feet long—it looked like a toy compared to the bar that stood in its way. Under Captain Dempsey's pilotage it was lining up for its crossing. Jet shivered. All those tons of cargo, the lives aboard ship—and nothing but the pilot's word that safe waters lay ahead. She'd wanted to be on that bridge for so long, she couldn't remember not wanting it, but today—right this moment—Jet was grateful for the years that would lie between her and her first command.

38

THE COAST GUARD helicopter set down at the air station on the far side of Youngs Bay, away from all the regatta events in town. The crew waited until the rotors stopped and then slid open the door. Jet's dad stepped out of the air-station office.

"Helmsman Ellstrom!" he bellowed, crossing the ground between them with long strides. "What would I tell your mother?!" He scooped her up in a hug as if she were younger than Oliver. His growl completely stopped working. "If I lost you . . . my Jet," he whispered in her ear.

Jet held him and squeezed her eyes shut. He was her lighthouse; she'd always know where he stood. The stress of the day drained away as Jet leaned her head against his shoulder. Eventually he set her on the ground, cupped his hand under her chin, and gave her bruised face a stern look.

"You haven't taken up boxing, have you?" The growl was back.

"Boxing? No. Absolutely not. Promise. Swear!"

"Good! Because I am not explaining a boxing career to your mother!"

He walked them over to a bench at the edge of the bay, sat down heavily, and patted the spot beside him. Jet kicked off her wet shoes and shrugged out of her life jacket.

"Well, out with it."

Dad fixed his gaze on the water, leaned his elbows on his knees, and clasped his hands together, a pose Jet recognized as one she took herself when she felt like hitting somebody and was trying not to. Any thought she'd had about bragging about the daring rescue she had pulled off flew right out of her head.

"I sailed into the shipping lane," she said, barely louder than a whisper. Jet felt her pride tug her to make an excuse, to explain that she'd been following a more important objective than the rules of right-of-way. She pushed those thoughts away. Her dad knew all about pride. He wanted the truth.

"I should have yielded to the larger vessel, and I didn't," she went on. "I sailed too close. I lost the wind. I struck a container ship. I abandoned the *Saga* and made an unauthorized boarding of a commercial vessel." Jet pulled her knees up to her chest and hugged them tight. "I sank your boat. It's gone. I'm sorry."

"Anything else?"

Jet rested her head on her knees. Ran over the events of the race. Thought through them again. And when she understood, it was like a slap she didn't see coming.

Kai.

Aunt Hanako and Uncle Lars were following the race. The entire staff at the power plant was rooting for him. They were waiting by their computers for pictures and texts to come in. The final casualty reports had been made for the earthquake and tsunami: Twenty-seven of those lost were children. This race was Uncle Lars's and Aunt Hanako's day off, their reason to cheer, their reminder of happier summers. Jet felt like she'd swallowed sand.

"I put Kai in danger," she said hoarsely. "I had no right. Not even to save someone else's life."

"See that you don't forget it."

"Never."

Jet rubbed her nose on the back of her hand. Her first shot at captaining a race, and she'd risked her crew. What if it had all gone wrong? She'd thrown the dice without thinking once about Kai's safety or his family. She stole a look at her dad. He wasn't any older than her friends' fathers, but he was grayer and more wrinkly. All his rowdiness after a rough bar crossing, his bluster and jokes, they had seemed childish to her before. She could see now how they helped him let go of the weight of command. The familiar sound track of wind and water played as she and her dad sat side by side.

"My Jet," he said. "I've lost you already, haven't I?"

"Lost me?"

"To the sea," he said. He gave a heavy sigh.

In all her dreaming about a life at sea, it had been easy not to think about her mom, sitting at the drawing table, watching the weather, and wondering if her girl was safe. If Jet made her own dreams come true, her parents would never be free of worrying. Jet would need years of at-sea time before she could even try for a piloting spot in Astoria. Her command could happen anywhere in the world. It could happen

in places where it was much harder to be a woman in a man's job.

"You could be anything, you know," Dad said. "You're smart, you're a hard worker, your grades are pretty good in spite of that little daydreaming habit you've got."

He gave her a sidelong glance. Jet rolled her eyes. Her teachers were always accusing her of daydreaming.

"There are easier ways to make a living," Dad went on. "You could become a doctor, even a surgeon, in less time than it will take you to become a bar pilot."

"I know."

"You know that in spite of Captain Dempsey's outstanding record, there are still people who think a woman has no place at the helm of a ship?"

Jet felt her face flush. "Is that why you want Kai to be the pilot?"

"Ah," Dad said, standing up, "your great-grandfather's compass."

Jet scrubbed her nose with her fist and walked to the water's edge.

"Your grandpa Lars's compass," he said with particular emphasis on the name. "My brother asked me to keep it for him when he joined the navy." He took

259

a few steps closer to Jet. "Compasses aren't useful in a submarine, and it was too precious to risk losing. I've been keeping it for his child—son or daughter—all these years because I promised him I would."

Jet took a step away from her dad, ashamed at her tears. Knowing she had no right to it didn't make her want the compass less. She wanted—needed—one solid thing to prove her ambition justified no matter how hard it would be to win a bar pilot's license in the end. He dropped a hand on Jet's shoulder and turned her toward him.

"But even if the compass was mine to give," he said, gently, "I'd see it in Kai's hand before yours. Look at you. You know exactly where you want to go in life. Do you have any idea how rare that is? How lucky?"

He lifted Jet's face and stroked away a tear.

"Your ambition is your true north, stronger than any magnet. I trust that force to bring you on the voyage that eventually"—Jet could see him calculating—"about thirty years from now, will bring you home to me and this bar and this pilotage." He smiled down at her. "And I pity the fool"—he placed a hand over his heart—"who tries to stand in your way."

Jet felt a glimmer of hope. Dad leaned closer and

whispered in her ear. "I'm not brave enough to stop you. Much as I'd like to try."

"And Kai?" Jet said.

"That cousin of yours," Dad said, "is adrift at the moment. The compass is just an invitation to think about a direction for his life. He might captain a ship someday. He'll be good at whatever he sets his mind to."

"He's the perfect crew," Jet said.

If he'd asked for command of the *Saga,* she'd have trusted him to do it right. For sure he'd have been more cautious.

"He's careful," Jet said, "and brave . . . and subtle." She smiled, remembering their first sail together.

Dad laughed. "Subtlety, yeah. I gotta get me some of that. It'd serve me well. Got any to spare?"

"None at all," Jet said. "Or so I hear."

The *Global Prosperity* had passed the mouth of Youngs Bay and was heading around Clatsop Spit, the last turn before the open ocean. When everything went smoothly, when every ship honored the right-of-way and the weather was fair, piloting a ship was like a dance between the tide and the current and the captain, a thing so beautiful you could forget for a moment how terrible it could be.

"I wish I wanted something easier," Jet said, "but I don't know how to make myself dream of something else."

"Your mom and I are never going to love the danger part. For the record, we don't love it that my brother and sister-in-law work with nuclear reactors, either. But if you're going to make your life on the water, you'd better have the best training you can get. So . . ." He gave Jet a stern look. "You provide the grades and the fitness scores, and I'll help you get a senator's nomination to the Merchant Marine Academy. You're going to have to work harder for this than you've ever worked in your life," he said.

The final horn from the end of the race and the faint sound of cheering drifted their way. They'd be giving out the prizes soon. Eight hours ago it would have killed her to lose, but now that championship cup hardly mattered.

"I know," Jet said. "I should probably make an effort not to sink any more ships."

"That's the spirit," Dad said.

He took her by the hand, and together they headed for the regatta.

39

AUNT KARIN AND Oliver ran toward Kai along
the dock. They both threw their arms around him,
laughing and crying and talking at once. Beck and his
parents were right behind them.

"Where's Jet?" Kai shouted, ready to turn the boat
around and go search for her.

"She's okay!" Beck yelled. "She made it!" He pointed
to the container ship that had caused all the trouble.
"She's right there."

The ship was a hundred yards from the finish
line. The coast guard helicopter hovered above it. On
top of the containers, standing alone, was Jet in her
orange life jacket and a white headband. The down-
wash whipped around her. She threw her hands up
and danced with excitement. Kai's jaw dropped to the

ground. He looked back toward the river, where he'd left Jet in the *Saga*. How did she get clear up there?

A surfman was lowered out of the helicopter to where Jet was standing.

"Oh, my baby girl," Aunt Karin groaned. She covered her eyes. "Tell me when it's over."

The surfman hooked Jet to a line and lifted her into the helicopter. Kai felt his stomach lurch as she swung and spiraled upward, but the crowd in the stands broke into a cheer, and Jet waved as if this was a stunt she'd pulled a thousand times before.

After the helicopter headed off in the direction of the coast guard air station, a crowd gathered around Beck and Kai. Roland was nowhere to be seen. Somebody called them heroes. Cameras flashed on all sides. The admiral of the regatta said something about the citizen-hero medal and a ceremony in the mayor's office next week. The newspaperman lined people up for pictures. The rescued boy's father came over. He shook Kai's hand so hard, Kai thought his arm would come off.

Aunt Karin was doing a video with her phone. "It's your parents," she said, pointing to the phone. "Say something to them!"

Kai bowed automatically and deeply, grateful that the gesture gave him a moment to compose his thoughts. He'd lost the race and his father's boat. He should apologize. He'd done it to save a boy's life, but he mustn't brag. He looked up as Aunt Karin panned the cheering crowd with her phone. He was mortified.

"Hey, Kai's mom and dad!" Beck shouted. He threw an arm over Kai's shoulder. "This guy is awesome! He's incredible!"

Kai barged in with a greeting in Japanese, hoping that his mother wouldn't think he had become an American bragger over the summer.

"This is my friend, Beck," he continued in Japanese. "A fellow sailor. There was an error in the race." Kai decided to gloss over the details about who was to blame. "Beck swam to this man's rescue." He gestured to the man who waved and said "thank you" over and over. "Beck kept him afloat until the coast guard came."

Kai turned to the boy. "This boy . . . ," he began but had to stop. His voice wouldn't make a sound. His grandparents were lost, and nothing he could do would bring them back. Aunt Karin took Kai by the arm and pulled him aside. She handed him the phone.

It wasn't a private moment, but it was the best they could do.

"The boy lived," Kai said. And he could see his mother cry. It was the good kind of crying.

"Your grandparents would be proud of you. You know they would," Kai's father said. "Listen, it's time for you to come home. Our work at the reactor is done. It's safe now."

He went on to explain that they'd found an apartment and a school in another town, where the tsunami had not reached. They wanted him home where he belonged. His mother dried her tears and told him a plane ticket would be waiting for him in a few days.

Kai's head was still spinning with thoughts of leaving when he took his place in the stands for the award ceremony. Beck and Skye and Bridgie joined him, but Roland sat at the far end of the stands with his parents. Nobody talked to them.

"Serves him right," Beck said quietly. "They disqualified the *Viking*. For failing to yield the right-of-way and endangering another boat."

"Is that what you two were yelling about?" Kai asked.

"He wouldn't listen to me," Beck said. "Once we made that turn around the last island and the current and the wind were in our favor, all he could see was the win. He pulled the tiller out of my hand." Beck was still speaking quietly, but Kai could feel his anger. "And that other boat? He didn't try to cut them off. He just forgot to look."

Beck glared at Roland with complete contempt. Skye, who had been flirting with Roland for weeks, wouldn't even look at him. A few minutes later she and Bridgie jumped up to smother Jet in a hug. They cooed over her courage and demanded a full account of her adventure, especially the helicopter part. Kai sat back, expecting to hear her tell the girls the fully embellished tale, but to his surprise Jet put them off and slipped in beside him just as the regatta officials took the stage.

Everyone quieted down for the awards ceremony. The Regatta Admiral called the winning team up to the stage. He handed them the Treasure Island Cup, and the pair held it aloft while cameras flashed.

The *Saga* could have won. They had a clear lead. Kai wanted to apologize. Jet had wanted this win for

a long time. She'd worked hard for it. She was the best helmsman in the race by a nautical mile. She deserved the win. Kai turned to her. She leaned in close.

"If you even think about apologizing to me, I'm going to pick up this entire grandstand and whack you over the head with it."

Yeah, that was his captain talking. Kai smiled and let it go. He let the whole thing go.

After the awards ceremony, everyone crowded around with more congratulations for the brave rescue. Oliver was nowhere in sight. Kai went looking for him and found him under the grandstand, pretend sword in hand, fighting the forces of evil. When Oliver caught sight of Kai, he selected an invisible battle ax from his mental inventory and handed it over.

"Mom says you're going back to Japan," he said.

Kai nodded.

"But you live here."

Kai had never expected to miss his cousins or this town. He wanted to go and he didn't. There was still so much work to do back home. There would be funerals, and it was almost time for the *Obon* festival. His parents needed them to be together again. Astoria

didn't feel like home. Not quite. Not yet. But it felt like a place he could belong.

"I've got some monsters to deal with over there," he said at last.

"But what about these monsters?" Oliver gestured to the ring of imaginary creatures around them.

Kai gripped his invisible weapon in both hands, lifted it over his head, and fought by Oliver's side until every last dragon was dead.

40

THE PICNIC AFTER the regatta was exactly like every other that Jet had been to her whole life. A bonfire was kindled. Music was made. Stories were told, and the celebrating went on long past sundown.

At first Jet was happy that Roland was no longer the center of attention in her group of friends. Beck was so angry with Roland's recklessness that he'd told him they'd never sail together again. Skye, who came from a big family of fishermen, was so mortified that Roland cut off somebody's right-of-way and nearly killed him that she'd had a friend of a friend break up with him on her behalf. It was terrific. It was like old times.

And yet.

Jet couldn't help remembering her own mistakes at

the beginning of the summer. It wasn't easy to make the right call out on the water. She thought she was going to die of shame for running the *Saga* aground in Youngs Bay, but at least she hadn't done it in front of her whole town. There was no getting around it. Roland had done a stupid thing, a dangerous thing. He'd never live it down. And Jet knew exactly how he felt.

She caught a glimpse of him leaving the picnic with his parents, and on an impulse she ran to cut them off at the parking lot.

"Hey," she said, and then wished she'd thought this through before she'd come over. Jet didn't want to be Roland's friend. He was just as awful as she'd always known him to be. If it weren't for his ego, his stupidity, she'd still have the *Saga*.

Even so.

"You sailed the *Viking* home all by yourself." Jet looked past him to the marina, where all the boats, except hers, were tied up for the night. "I bet that was hard."

"Yeah," Roland mumbled. He was looking for an attack. Jet could tell. It was tempting.

But.

"That boat means a lot to Beck and Captain

271

Chandler. So thanks." Jet took a deep breath and thought it through. Yup. That was all she wanted to say to him. She turned and dashed back to her friends.

A HALF–DOZEN MARSHMALLOWS and two burned fingers later, Jet turned to Beck and Kai, who'd lingered around the fire long after the others had gone off to play flashlight tag.

"We should make wish boats. Like we did at outdoor school." She polished off the last bite of her s'more and wiped her sticky fingers on her jeans.

"Wish boats?" Kai lifted his marshmallow out of the fire.

"It's a summer-camp thing," Beck said, "for remembering a good time." He handed Kai the last of the chocolate and graham crackers. Kai expertly slid the marshmallow off its stick like he'd been making s'mores all his life.

"We need candles," Jet added.

She rooted around in the remains of the picnic supplies and scooped up three tea lights. They crossed under the Astoria Bridge and dropped down into a small sandy cove on the edge of the Columbia.

"There's plenty of driftwood," Jet said. She swept

her flashlight over a tangle of weathered bark and branches. "This would make a good boat." She handed a foot-long section of cedar bark to Kai and took a similar piece for herself. "And then you can decorate it however you want."

Jet looked around until she found a beach rose to decorate her boat with. Kai took out a pocketknife to carve something. Beck wove a raft from sticks and sword ferns, then walked along the water looking for shells. When he was out of earshot, Jet went over and sat in the circle of light beside Kai. It was the first moment they'd had alone since the race that morning.

"Oliver said you're going home."

Kai nodded. He didn't look up from his carving. Jet looked over his shoulder. He was carving words in Japanese. He didn't pull away, so Jet leaned back and waited for him to talk. The constant rush of the river and the hum of the fish cannery gave them both a cover for saying nothing. There were things Jet wanted to say. And for once in her life, she wanted to say them carefully.

While she was still choosing words, Kai turned his wish boat toward her, tapped the first of the characters with the tip of his knife, and said, "Obā-san."

Jet was going to say something about the race, but Kai's single word stopped her in her tracks. She and Kai had poured all their energy into the race for a whole month. Sails every morning, practice with the GPS after lunch, study of the river charts at night. It's good for him, she'd told herself. I'm helping him forget his troubles. But maybe, maybe all this time, he'd been wanting to remember.

"You're going home for the funeral," she said.

Kai kept carving, slowly, carefully. He paused from time to time to blow the little chips of bark away from his work. Jet wanted to hug him, but he'd hate that. All she knew of her own grandparents were pictures and stories. They'd died before her mom and dad got married. She couldn't even imagine what it would be like to lose the people you'd gone to every day after school. It would be like losing the parents you knew better than your own parents. More than the night breeze made her shiver. Jet zipped up her jacket and stuffed her hands in her pockets.

The one image from their adventures of the day that wouldn't leave her head was not crashing into the ship or making the jump. It was the moment she and Kai had pulled alongside the *Blue Dolphin*. The boy inside

was so small—peanut-butter smear on his face, dinosaur on his life jacket, and complete terror in his eyes. And then Kai had said, "We'll make it home."

Home.

And just for a second, Jet saw hope light him up. Kai was busy boarding. He didn't see. But she couldn't shake the look of him. That boy had thought he was lost, and Kai had saved him. Jet wanted to do something for Kai. Say something. Shout something. Something like, Hey, you big dope! You saved somebody's life!

That would be the wrong thing to say. She curled her arms around her knees and waited for something better to occur to her.

"He said run," Kai said quietly. "But I wouldn't do it. I was so sure I could save them. I thought I'd taken them far enough." He looked at the lights across the river. "And then the water kept coming and coming, and Ojī-san said, 'Don't make her watch you die. Please.'"

Kai's voice dropped to a whisper. "So I ran. I didn't look back. Not one time."

Jet stole a look at her cousin. He wasn't crying. He was a person who'd run out of tears. Jet felt full of them, but she forced them back. It would only make

him feel worse to see her cry. She waited until her voice was free from wobbles.

"Did they see you run?"

After a long silence, Kai nodded.

"So at least you gave him his last wish."

Kai didn't answer. Jet was in danger of hugging him, but just in time Beck's flashlight came closer. Jet dug into her pocket for the candles.

"One for your grandma and one for your grandpa," she whispered before Beck could hear.

Kai took both candles and set them gently on his wish boat.

Beck set his elaborately decorated raft on the sand and settled in beside Jet. His raft was loaded down with shells and leaves and twigs, as if the pile of them could equal the size of the wish Jet knew he would be making. Her own biggest wish seemed tiny compared to wanting your dad to walk again. Jet handed him the last candle. Beck lit them. He put one of his mussel shells and an empty crab claw onto Jet's boat so it wouldn't be so plain without a candle. They pushed their wish boats into the river, and the rising tide kept them turning in a slow circle in the cove at the edge of the river's deeper currents.

"Well, Captain," Beck said. "Speech?"

"Yeah," Kai said, turning to Jet. "What do you have to say for yourself, Captain of the *Saga*?"

"Oh my gosh," Jet said, burying her face in her hands. All the things she'd wanted to say before rushed back. "Our boat. Our dads' boat! I'm so sorry, Kai."

"Now how are we going to teach Oliver to sail?" Kai said.

"I know. I'm really, really sorry!"

"That's pretty optimistic!" Beck said. "How many times do you think you can patch a boat that old?"

"Patch it!" Jet said. "Oh, come on, Oliver wouldn't run it aground. He's a better sailor than that."

"He does like to engage pirates, though," Kai said.

Jet imagined Oliver at the helm, mainsheet in one hand and cutlass in the other. It was a fair point. The boy was a shipwreck waiting to happen.

Beck laughed. "We're going to have to make up some rules about pirates. But we'll make good crew out of him, you'll see."

"He's going to have a good teacher, anyway," Kai said.

"You could teach a mollusk to sail," Beck added.

"If only I had a boat," Jet said.

"There'll be other boats," Beck said. "Better boats."

"She was pretty, though," Jet said wistfully. "Do you think it's bad karma to sink your very first command?"

Beck nodded vigorously. "Very bad karma."

"Your future at sea is doomed," Kai said with a smile. "Unless you carry a very special good-luck charm with you at all times."

"A charm?"

"I have just the thing."

Kai dug in his pocket and put the charm in her hand. It was round and heavy. Jet didn't have to look to know what it was.

"Kai, it's yours. Dad wanted you to have it. Your father was saving it for you."

"If it's mine, then it's mine to give."

"But—"

"Please!" Kai closed her hand around their great-grandfather's compass. "Just hold on to it until next summer. You can give it back to me then."

"You're coming back?" Jet said.

"Well, yes," Kai said, a little flustered. "I mean, I didn't ask my parents yet because they're still kind of busy, but they'll say yes . . . because . . . because I'll

figure out how to make them say yes. Because I want to be here just as much as I want to be there."

He opened the lid of the compass that was still in Jet's outstretched hand. The dial swung left and then right, settling with the gold arrow pointing across the Columbia.

"And in the meantime, I'll be right . . . here." He pointed to the mark on the dial. "Two hundred sixty degrees west by south."

"But what about you?" Jet said. "Don't you want this for when you're a captain, too? There are maritime academies in Japan, right?"

"Best ones in the world!" Kai grinned.

"Oh, I don't know about that," Jet said, warming up her arguments. Kai saw it coming and held up a hand in surrender.

"Take your maritime academy. I don't want to command ships. I want to make them."

"Really?" Beck said.

Kai nodded enthusiastically. "Sailing ships," he said.

"Are you going to race them?" Jet said, plans already brewing.

"Maybe, if I can find a helmsman with a little more sense of responsibility. Respect for my handiwork." He nudged her on the shoulder.

"Shut up!" Jet said, nudging him back. "That ship outweighed me by, like, eight million pounds! What was I supposed to do?"

The three of them launched into a heated argument about sailing tactics, and as they bickered and laughed and drew out strategy diagrams in the sand, the tide turned. Their wish boats caught the outgoing current, slipped out of the cove, and headed for the open ocean.

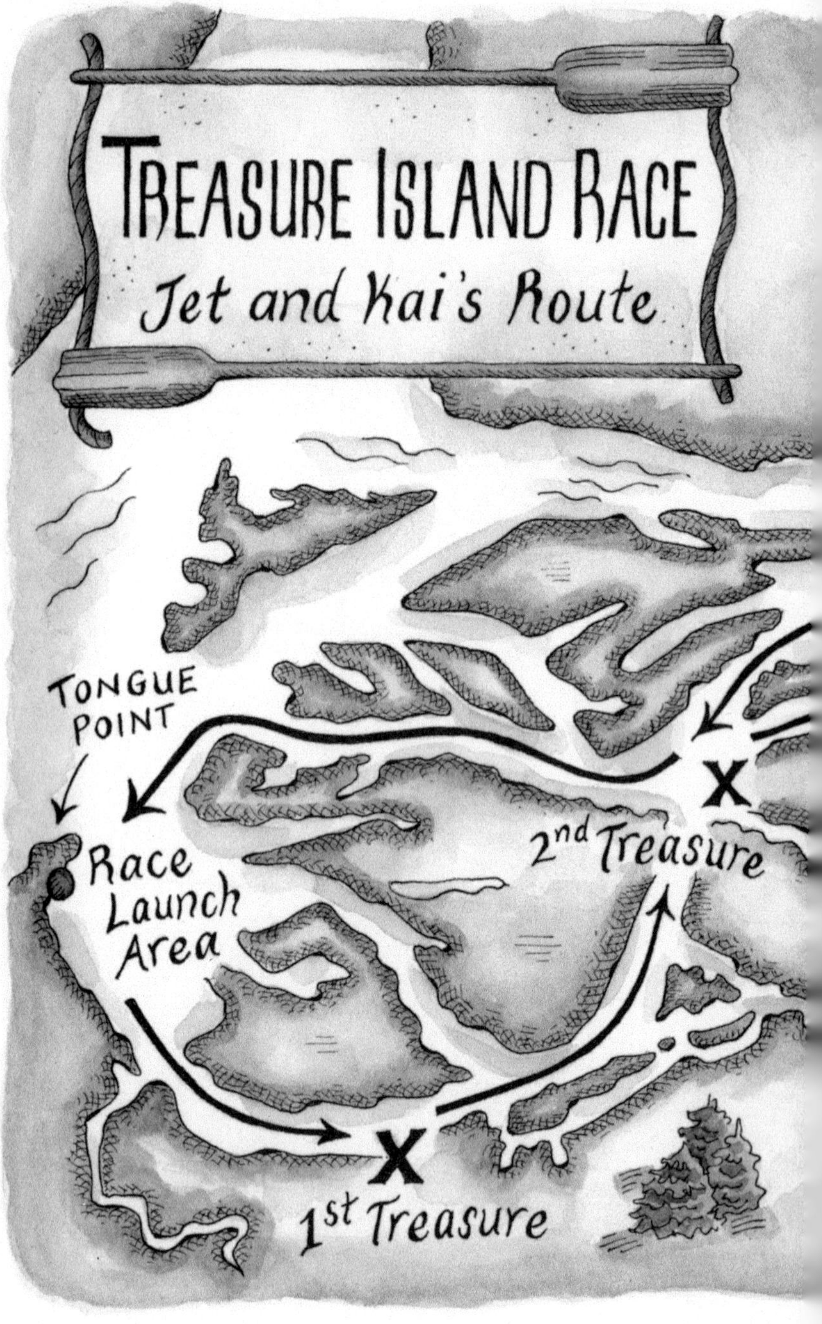
TREASURE ISLAND RACE
Jet and Kai's Route
TONGUE POINT
Race Launch Area
1st Treasure
2nd Treasure

A Message for Young Mariners

To go to sea is not for everyone, and in a profession dominated by men, it certainly seems like an unlikely career path for women. It is a lifestyle with long periods of time away from home and requires juggling family and a normal home life with work. But it is all possible now.

That was not always the case, however. We can thank a handful of brave women who were lighthouse keepers and rescued sailors in the 1860s, like Ida Lewis of Rhode Island. More recently, the women who attended the country's maritime academies in the 1970s—when it was still considered "not a girl job"—paved the way for future women. Today it is normal to have women enrolled at the maritime academies and working aboard ship.

Going to sea can mean the wonder of visiting ports around the world, witnessing different cultures, and seeing countries as a working sailor rather than as a tourist. It can mean following your passion, living your love for being on the water, and finding your place. "Breaking the barrier" may at first seem impossible for Jet, but it is not so difficult anymore. Today the option is there for everyone.

The opportunity to follow your dreams and ambitions and to develop your own sea stories is important. You can "sail like a girl" and be successful. As Per says to his daughter, Jet, "Ambition is your true north." What a wonderful vision! No one can fail when being true to themselves—when following their true north.

Captain Deborah Dempsey
Columbia River Bar Pilot (1994–2012)

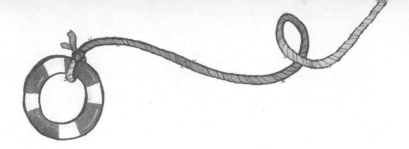

Author's Note

COLUMBIA BAR AND CAPTAIN DEMPSEY

The Columbia Bar is the most dangerous passage in the Pacific. More than two thousand vessels and seven hundred souls have been lost over the bar in recorded history. The first bar pilot was Comcomly, a chief of the Chinook tribe, which has lived at the mouth of the Columbia River for many centuries. In 1816, he began guiding sailing ships over the bar from a canoe. Members of the Hudson's Bay Company also provided early pilotage. The current bar pilots' association formed in 1846, making it one of the oldest continually operating businesses in Oregon. There are sixteen bar pilots, all with an unlimited Master Mariner's license that qualifies them to captain any ship of any kind in the world. It takes decades of at-sea time to gain this qualification. These pilots take three thousand to four thousand ships over the bar every year, which bring approximately 40 million tons of cargo into the ports of Oregon and Washington.

All the characters in this book are fictional except for Captain Deborah Dempsey. She was the first woman to graduate from a U.S. maritime academy, the first to carry a Master Mariner's license and command cargo ships in international waters, and in 1994 the first woman ever to pilot the Columbia Bar. She retired from her pilotage after eighteen years and now teaches part-time at a maritime academy and shares her love of small-craft sailing at the Community Boating Center in Bellingham, Washington. She is a masterful teller of sea stories.

SAILING

The Astoria Regatta has been a regular summer festival in Oregon since 1894. It features many boating events, but the Treasure Island Race is my own invention. As far as I know, nobody runs a sailboat race that uses geo-caching. As I've imagined it, the race takes place upriver, away from the very dangerous conditions over the Colum-bia Bar in the more sheltered waters of the Lewis and Clark National Wildlife Refuge. The course I've laid out on the map would likely take a little longer than it does in the story. Throughout the book I've tried to be accu-rate to the local conditions and true to the sailing terms without being overly technical. Everything Jet and Kai do on the water is possible, but some of it would take an

extra helping of both skill and luck. If you're curious about how sailing works, there is a terrific sailing simulator by National Geographic that shows how the wind and sails interact to make a boat move: nationalgeographic.com/volvooceanrace/interactives/sailing/index.html.

Glossary of Sailing Terms

beat: to sail upwind, which requires zigzagging back and forth

catamaran: a racing sailboat with twin hulls and usually a cloth deck

cleat: a device for securing a line

course: the direction in which the boat is pointed

dinghy: a small open boat that can be sailed or rowed

downwind: the direction the wind is going

helms alee: a warning to the crew that the boat is making a tack

helmsman: the crew member who steers

port: the left side of the boat looking forward

ready about: a command to the crew to get ready to make a tack

rig: to prepare a boat for sailing by raising the mast and readying the sails

run: to sail downwind, which can be done without zigzagging

shackle: a device for attaching a sheet to a sail

ship oars: a command to the crew to stop rowing and secure the oars

starboard: the right side of the boat looking forward

tack: to turn the nose of the boat through the wind in order to make a zigzag course; as the bow turns, the mainsail swings across the boat, which means the crew must duck to avoid being hit by the boom

trim the sail: to adjust the sail's angle for maximum speed

upwind: the direction the wind is coming from

wing and wing: to sail downwind with the mainsail and jib sail on opposite sides of the boat

TSUNAMIS

The tsunami at the beginning of the story is a fictional event, although a similar, larger earthquake and tsunami struck the northern coast of Japan on March 11, 2010. A tsunami forms when an underwater volcanic eruption, landslide, or earthquake sends massive amounts of energy through the ocean. As this flow of energy approaches the shallow water along a shore, the energy becomes concentrated, and a powerful wave is created. Tsunami waves can be as tall as one hundred feet and move as quickly as six hundred miles per hour. A tsunami has incredible

destructive power, crushing and sweeping away everything in its path. Fortunately, NOAA (the National Oceanic and Atmospheric Administration) runs the Pacific Tsunami Warning Center, which detects underwater earthquakes and spreads the warning to communities in the path of dangerous waves.

Geocaching

The Global Positioning System (GPS) is a network of satellites that orbit the earth and beam down signals, which can be used to pinpoint position, speed, and time. On May 2, 2000, GPS became available to the public, and one day later a man from Oregon decided to test how well the system worked by hiding a box of "treasures" near his home in Beaver Creek. He posted the coordinates of the box so that fellow GPS enthusiasts could find it using a GPS tracker. Dozens did, and a new sport was born. Anyone can play; all you need is a sense of adventure and a GPS device (which can be loaded as an app on many phones). There is a website for logging treasures that you've hidden and for getting the coordinates for treasures to find. More than six million people are geocachers, and hidden treasures can be found in hundreds of countries all over the world. There's probably one near you right now. You can learn lots more about geocaching on geocaching.com.

RECOMMENDED BOOKS

If you enjoyed this story, you will love the Swallows and Amazons series by Arthur Ransome, about four siblings who spend their summers sailing in England's Lake District.

Graham Salisbury wrote a story about a Boy Scout troop that survives an earthquake and tsunami on the Big Island of Hawaii. *Night of the Howling Dogs* is a gripping read and is based on a true story.

Tomo: Friendship Through Fiction—An Anthology of Japan Teen Stories is a collection of stories about being a Japanese or bicultural teenager in the midst of the tragic events of the 2011 Sendai earthquake. It was edited by Holly Thompson, and a portion of the proceeds go to relief for children displaced by the tsunami.

For more information about bar pilots, read "Steering Ships Through a Treacherous Waterway" by Matt Jenkins, *Smithsonian Magazine,* February 2009. If you are looking for an introduction to sailing, *The Complete Sailor* by David Seidman is a comprehensive and readable guide with lots of useful illustrations.

RECOMMENDED POEMS

There are many poems about the sea. Here are four that I read while working on this story.

Emily Dickinson never went to sea but beautifully captured in eight brief lines the longing of a landsman for open water in her poem "Exultation is the going."

Alfred Lord Tennyson wrote "Crossing the Bar," a poem that many seafarers can quote from memory and whose last lines are sometimes found on a sailor's grave.

Robert Louis Stevenson is best known for his novel *Treasure Island,* but he also wrote poetry, including a ballad about a sailor struggling with bad weather and rough seas between two headlands much like the Columbia Bar. It's called "Christmas at Sea."

Poetry has a long, rich history in Japan. In the aftermath of the Sendai earthquake, I often heard reference to a poem by Kenji Miyazawa called "Be Not Defeated by the Rain." I particularly like the translation by David Sulz. It has much to say about Japanese values and culture.

Acknowledgments

Hearty thanks to my agent, Stephen Fraser, who has piloted this and all my stories over the bar of the publishing process, in foul weather and fair. I am lucky to have his steady hand at the helm.

This book had a long voyage on its way to the page. Many thanks to my editors—Jim Thomas, who was there from the start, and Michelle Nagler and Jenna Lettice, who brought the story home. The entire crew at Random House did a beautiful job with all the details of design and placement—my particular thanks to Casey Lloyd, Liz Tardiff, and Alison Kolani. And to Julie McLaughlin for the vibrant cover art.

I am grateful to my critique group for their support over many years: Cheryl Coupe, Mike Gettle-Gilmartin, Cliff Lehman, Lyra Knierem, Barbara Lyles, Nora Ericson, Robin Herrera, and Amy Baskin.

Early in my research process, I heard Captain Debbie Dempsey speak about her career as the first woman pilot on the Columbia Bar. She was generous and supportive from the start in answering my questions and correcting my errors and offering a heartfelt message to my readers. It is not easy to be an ambitious woman in this world, but she manages to be fiercely professional, dauntless, and kind. I hope she will inspire many an adventure-hungry girl to be a little bolder. She has certainly inspired me.

I'm grateful to the Child Lit discussion group moderated by Michael Joseph of Rutgers University, which has led to many fruitful connections in my writing life. In the case of this book, I found James Kennedy, former resident of Japan, who introduced me to Zack Davisson, who researches and translates Japanese ghost stories. Zack helped me understand my characters' fears in greater cultural context.

Misao Sundahl and Holly Thompson also helped me understand the language and cultural context of a child growing up in Japan.

I'm grateful to Nicholas McGowen for answering my questions about coast guard operations, small boat safety, and navigational conditions on the Columbia River. Jonathan Parry provided helpful information about the navy.

Thank you to my first reader, Colette Parry, for her generous readings and insightful suggestions. Thank you to my husband, Bill, for his very spontaneous purchase of a beautiful but dilapidated sailboat many years ago. He mended it, and together with our children we learned how to sail, which has made our lives richer and wilder and more beautiful than before.

And finally, thank you to Ursula K. Le Guin, who wrote *A Wizard of Earthsea,* a story Bill and I loved from our childhoods, a story that made us long for a little sailboat and a life full of big adventures.

About the Author

Rosanne Parry is always searching for the perfect wind in her sailboat, the *Selkie;* the perfect word in her treehouse writing studio; and the perfect book for patrons at Annie Bloom's Books. She is the author of *Heart of a Shepherd, Second Fiddle,* and *Written in Stone.* Rosanne lives with her family in Portland, Oregon. Visit her at RosanneParry.com.